The Billionaire Bentleys 3

Von Diesel

Lock Down Publications and Ca$h
Presents
The Billionaire Bentleys
A Novel by *Von Diesel*

The Billionaire Bentleys

Lock Down Publications
P.O. Box 944
Stockbridge, Ga 30281
www.lockdownpublications.com

Lock Down Publications
Like our page on Facebook: Lock Down Publications
@
www.facebook.com/lockdownpublications.ldp

Book interior design by: **Shawn Walker**
Edited by: **Shamika Smith**

Stay Connected with Us!

Text **LOCKDOWN** to 22828 to stay up-to-date with
new releases, sneak peaks, contests and more…
Thank you!

Submission Guideline.

Submit the first three chapters of your completed manuscript to ldpsubmissions@gmail.com, subject line: Your book's title. The manuscript must be in a .doc file and sent as an attachment. Document should be in Times New Roman, double spaced and in size 12 font. Also, provide your synopsis and full contact information. If sending multiple submissions, they must each be in a separate email.

Have a story but no way to send it electronically? You can still submit to LDP/Ca$h Presents. Send in the first three chapters, written or typed, of your completed manuscript to:

LDP: Submissions Dept
P.O. Box 944
Stockbridge, Ga 30281

DO NOT send original manuscript. Must be a duplicate.

Provide your synopsis and a cover letter containing your full contact information.

Thanks for considering LDP and Ca$h Presents.

Von Diesel

Chapter One

Shemika, Famous, and Camryn had just returned from the corner coffee shop where Camryn had consumed two hamburgers, a strawberry milkshake, and a dish of chocolate ice cream when Nancy appeared at the front door.

"Mother!" Shemika exclaimed. "What are you doing here?"

Nancy looked from Famous to Camryn, then back at her daughter. "Perhaps if you answered your phone, I wouldn't have been forced to drag myself over here," she said, in an extremely pissed-off tone.

"Oh, God! I'm sorry," Shemika said. Lowering her voice, she added, "With the tragedy and all, I've just been so busy. Touch is in a state. He asked me to take Camryn, so I did. Fortunately, Famous came along to help because—"

"Hey, Mrs. Scott-Simon," Famous said, coming up behind Shemika.

"Good evening," Nancy responded with a frosty nod.

"Uh, I'm gonna put the movie on for Camryn," he said. "Is that okay?"

"Thanks," Shemika replied, realizing how this must look to Nancy. "Let's go into the kitchen, Mom," she said, leading her mother away.

Tight-lipped, Nancy followed her daughter into the kitchen.

"You do realize what this means?" Nancy said, fussily brushing off one of the kitchen stools with her hand before perching uncomfortably on it.

"Yes, Mom," Shemika said patiently. "It means that Camryn has lost her mother, so I'm looking after her because her nanny quit and—"

"Shemika!" Nancy interrupted sternly. "We have to cancel the wedding."

"Excuse me."

"We have to cancel the wedding," Nancy repeated, enunciating every word.

"Oh," Shemika said, sitting down. "Are you saying we should postpone it?"

"Postponing is not an option."

"Then maybe we should go ahead," Shemika said. "I'll talk to Touch. I'm sure he'll—"

"Shemika! Be silent. We are not barbarians. This man's wife—"

"Ex-wife, Mother."

"This man's ex-wife has been brutally murdered in the most appalling way, and our family name cannot be connected to this scandal. I will not allow it. You have to give Touch back the ring, break off the engagement, and leave town on an extended vacation."

"You're not serious?" Shemika said, feeling dizzy and confused.

"I am extremely serious," Nancy said. "You must distance yourself from the Bentley family before this appalling scandal ruins our good name."

"Mother, Touch is my fiancé. I am marrying him."

"No, Shemika, you're not."

"You can't tell me who I'm going to marry," Shemika said heatedly.

"Besides, Touch didn't kill his wife. He had nothing to do with it."

"How do you know that?"

"Oh, for God's sake, Mother."

"Have you been watching the news on TV?"

"No."

"They're showing pictures of Touch and mentioning you. I shudder to imagine what the newspapers will say tomorrow."

"Touch is an innocent victim here, Mother. He has no control over the press."

"He's not a victim, Shemika," Nancy said stiffly. "He's an extremely affluent, well-connected man whose wife has been brutally murdered, and the suspicion lies on him."

"That's nonsense, Mother."

"You have to cancel this wedding. I've discussed everything with our family lawyer, and he agrees. I'm expecting you to obey me, Shemika, and for God's sake, get that child and Touch's brother out of your apartment."

"You're crazy, Mother."

"I'm merely telling you what has to be done for your own protection. And you'd better do it, young lady. Otherwise, I will be forced to speak to your grandmother about your inheritance." And with that, Nancy was on her feet. "I expect to hear from you later," she said, making a grand exit.

***

Touch drove into the underground parking basement of Sadiya's building, buzzed up to the front desk, and spoke to the desk clerk. "Mr. Bentley here," he said. "Are the press still outside?"

"Yes, sir, they've been around all day."

"How about the police?"

"Most of them have left. I believe there's one cop stationed outside the, uh, late Mrs. Bentley's apartment."

"You're sure?"

"Yes, sir. Irena, Mrs. Bentley's personal maid, tried to get in earlier to fetch some of her things, but the cop wouldn't allow her access."

"Right," Touch said slowly. "Well, I do need to get in to collect my daughter's clothes. See if you can offer the cop some refreshments."

"I shouldn't think he's allowed to leave his post, sir."

"Offer him something. I'm sure you can convince him to take a break."

"I'll try."

"You do that, and I'll make it worth your while."

"I'll see what I can do."

Touch waited five minutes before taking the elevator up to the apartment. The doorman had done his job. There was no cop present, so he ducked under the yellow police tape and let himself in with the key he'd never relinquished.

He slipped inside the marble foyer, shut the door behind him, and stood there for a moment, images of Sadiya's body flashing before his eyes. Soon, he realized he'd better move fast.

He recalled that Sadiya had kept a locked box in the top of a closet in the guestroom. "It is where I keep jewelry that's not in the bank," she'd once informed him when he'd caught her hiding the box. He'd never bothered to check. He'd believed her. Why wouldn't he?

He went straight to the guestroom closet, moved a few things around, and located the box. In case the cop was back, he hurried into Camryn's room, scooped up an armful of clothes and a few stuffed animals, and let himself out.

The policeman was still not there. Touch had said it was going to be such a problem, but he'd found it an easy task.

Now he planned on spending the rest of the evening discovering whatever information he could about his deceased ex-wife because he was convinced that she'd had secrets, and he was determined to find out what they were.

Chapter Two

This is your shot, Velvet, do not blow it.

Bruce's words kept swimming around in her head as she sat on a plane, making its way to L.A. She'd taken a leap of faith and decided to go for it. This was a difficult decision because she hadn't wanted to miss her meeting with Tristin and the producer that he'd promised to set her up with. She was into that more than anything, but how could she turn down the kind of money she'd make doing the modeling job? Not to mention a trip to L.A., a place she'd only ever dreamed about.

This was a once-in-a-lifetime chance she couldn't refuse. It was a huge break that could lead to so many other opportunities.

And yet, she'd been torn about blowing off the meeting with Tristin's producer because, above all else, singing was her passion.

She'd left a message on Tristin's private cell informing him of her situation, hoping he'd understand and reschedule. In the meantime, she'd barely had time to throw some things into a bag and get herself to the airport.

This was her first plane ride, and she was quite apprehensive. The sour-faced woman sitting next to her in the window seat did not seem inclined to talk, so Velvet buckled her seatbelt, sat back, and prepared to enjoy the ride.

She realized she hadn't called her mom back, and then she started thinking about Malshonda. How was she supposed to reach her? Malshonda had promised to call her with a phone number, but she was obviously too busy settling in with Slick Jimmy. If the plane crashed, the only person who would know she was on it was Bruce, a man she'd met only once. And Tristin, because of the message she'd left him.

Suddenly, she felt guilty. She should've called Fatima back. It was bad energy to hold grudges, and at least she now knew the truth about her father. She made up her mind that once she reached the hotel, she'd call her mom, along with Aaron and Peaches at the coffee shop, to inform them she wasn't coming back. If she could make this kind of money, it was dumb not to take advantage of the opportunity. She felt bad about her Ragtags. They must be wondering what had happened to her. The moment she got paid, she promised herself that she'd drop them off some cash. That way, they could buy their own food.

Once again, she started wondering what the shoot was for. Something fun, she hoped. She should've asked Bruce, but everything had happened so quickly, and he'd been in a rush, so she hadn't had a chance.

After a while, she fell asleep and didn't wake until the plane landed.

Outside the gate, she looked around until she spotted a middle-aged black man holding up a white card with her name on it. Hurrying over to him, she said, "Uh, I think you're here for me?" making it sound like a question.

"Velvet?"

"That's right."

"I'm your driver, ma'am," he said politely. "The car is parked outside. Do you have baggage?"

"Only the bag I'm carrying."

"I'll take that for you," he said, relieving her of the heavy bag filled with anything she'd been able to stuff in at such short notice.

A car and a driver? This was majorly cool! Malshonda would have a jealous fit when she told her.

She followed the man outside to a white limo parked curbside. "Is this for me?" she asked, unable to hide her surprise. "Are you sure?"

"Yes, ma'am," he said, holding open the door. "I'm driving you to Shutters."

"That's a hotel, right?"

"Yes, ma'am. It's in Santa Monica by the ocean."

This was too much. The only time she'd visited the ocean was one Sunday she'd spent at Coney Island when she was fourteen. She hadn't enjoyed the experience. The beach was packed with sweaty, half-naked people, a giant wave had nearly drowned her, and some annoying boy had got a sticky glob of cotton candy caught in her hair.

There was a phone in the car. She wondered if she was allowed to use it. No, best to wait until she got to the hotel. And how much would phone calls cost from a hotel? Probably a fortune, although Bruce had said all expenses were taken care of, so maybe they wouldn't charge her.

The hotel was all white and quite glamorous. They were very welcoming to her at Reception and showed her to an ocean-front room with a small balcony overlooking the beach.

She looked around in amazement. The room was nicer than the apartment she shared with Malshonda. There was a mini-bar filled with miniature bottles of drinks and all kinds of delicious goodies, a flat-screen TV, a soft, luxurious bed, a bathroom with a walk-in shower, and a huge tub. Plus, there was another TV, and she was sure no roaches or rats were present!

Kicking off her shoes, she opened up the sliding doors, stepped out onto a small balcony, and took a deep breath. It was past midnight, but the air was balmy and the sound of the ocean soothingly loud.

I'm dreaming, she told herself. This is all some whacked-out crazy dream. Is this really happening to me?

A knock on the door jolted her back to reality. "Who is it?" she called out.

"It's Savage, your friendly neighborhood photographer," a male voice replied.

"Hold on a minute," she said, slipping on her shoes, then opening the door.

Standing there was the pizza boy from the elevator on her first go-see.

"What the—"

Before she could finish, Pizza Boy gave her a lopsided grin. "Never trust a man eating pizza in an elevator," he said, with a jaunty wink. "Turned out you were the fresh face my camera's gonna die for. You are gonna be on the cover of a major news magazine, so get a good night's sleep. Don't let me down tomorrow 'cause you're my choice, and the suits are all pissed they didn't get to check you out—six a.m. hair, makeup, and wardrobe will be on your doorstep. Put yourself in their hands 'cause they really know their shit."

"Oh, yeah," he added, with another goofy grin. Welcome to L.A." And as quickly as that, he was gone, leaving her in a state of total flux.

***

It turned out that Pizza Boy was one of the hottest photographers around. Only twenty-six, he'd already scored important covers on all the major magazines with his sexy original style reminiscent of the early Annie Leibovitz.

At the present time, he'd been hired to launch a new magazine, *White Cool*, aimed at the twenty- to forty-five-year-old male reader. He could've booked any one of the top models for the cover, but he'd been looking for someone totally new, and Velvet was that someone. Disillusioned with the familiar faces crowding his studio on the day Velvet had come in for her shoot, he'd grabbed a pizza and taken off to get some air, which was how he'd come to be sharing an elevator with her. He'd viewed her as incredibly beautiful and street smart with a streak of naïveté. He'd known immediately she was the one.

Now he had her posing on a beach in L.A., wearing a thong and a skimpy bra top in some kind of jungle print. There were shots of her leaning against a palm tree, her body oiled and glistening with wild exotic make-up and extensions in her hair.

She'd awoken way before six and rushed to check out the view from her room. Miles of white sand leading to the ocean, clumps of exotic palm trees, an expanse of clear blue sky, a jogging and bike path, where people were already out and about. Wow! It was Paradise. She still couldn't believe this was happening to her so fast.

The "team" stood around watching her every move as she posed for Savage's camera. The "team" consisted of Quinn, make-up artist supreme, a sleek black guy with shoulder-length white-blond hair and bleached eyebrows, Holliday, one of the best hair stylists in L.A., and Uma, a butch celebrity stylist with an impeccable eye for detail. They were a friendly trio who'd worked on her for two hours before Savage was satisfied.

Savage's "team" consisted of two energetic young assistants and a runner. There was also a catering team setting up lunch under hooded canopies further down the beach.

Savage had thought of everything to create the right atmosphere, he'd even set up his iPod with speakers, and sexy Brazilian music filled the air.

At first, she'd felt exposed and awkward. Then slowly, she'd begun to relax. Savage was so encouraging, and as soon as he felt she was ready, he showed her a series of pics he'd shot of her. She was secretly thrilled; she could hardly believe it was her.

After that, everything was easy, and she fell into the rhythm of posing seductively as if she'd done it a hundred times before.

"Bring it on!" Savage kept yelling at her. "You look incredible. Yeah! Bring it on, Velvet. That's it! Bring it on!"

By the time they broke for lunch, she was on a major high. The "team" swooped down on her. Uma slipped a white toweling robe around her shoulders while Holliday informed her that for the next set-up, everything would be entirely different, so she'd better eat fast as they had work to do.

Could it get any better?

She didn't think so.

Her adrenaline was pumping at an alarming rate. Last night she'd fallen asleep with all her clothes on. She'd lain on top of the bed for a second, and that was it, total wipe-out. She hadn't phoned anyone, and now she felt guilty because, like Malshonda, she'd let Peaches and Aaron down at the coffee shop. It wasn't fair to leave them two waitresses short with no explanation.

But what could she do? It was as if she was on an express train and couldn't get off. Hell, I didn't want to get off. It was all such a trip.

Lunch under the softly swaying palm trees was another trip: lobster and shrimp, mixed salads, an assortment of bread, wine, and music. Aunt Aretha would be in heaven.

Savage's runner brought him the L.A. edition of the New York Post. He proceeded to sit back and read the sports pages. Velvet's eye caught the garish headline on the front page.

MURDER IN MANHATTAN!
Society Wife Slain!
Sadiya Bentley Stabbed To Death!

Oh, wow! So that was why Fatima was trying to reach her.

"Can I use your phone?" she asked Holliday. "I think I'd better speak to my mom."

Von Diesel

Chapter Three

Sitting in his kitchen, scanning the newspapers, Touch realized the headlines were even worse than he could have imagined. "Society Wife Slain!" screamed the *New York Post*. "Society Beauty Stabbed Six Times!" was on the cover of the *Daily News*. Even the *New York Times* and the *Wall Street Journal* featured the story on their front pages. There were plenty of pictures, too, mostly of Sadiya at various events, and a few of her with Touch. There was even one of her with Camryn at a tennis tournament in the Hamptons.

"Damn!" Touch raged aloud. "Why do they have to put my daughter in the paper?"

At that moment, he realized he had not called Shemika. The night before, he'd been so busy going through the papers he'd found in Sadiya's locked box that he'd forgotten all about Shemika and Camryn.

He picked up the phone and called her. "I'm so sorry, sweetheart," he said apologetically. "I was exhausted. I must have passed out. Are you okay? Is Famous still there?"

"No," Shemika said. "He left as soon as Camryn fell asleep."

"How is she today?"

"Unhappy. She wants to be with you, Touch, and I can't blame her. Yesterday she went through a traumatic experience, and she needs to be with her daddy."

"Right now, it's difficult," he said, stalling because he had no idea what he was supposed to do with Camryn.

"Touch, she hardly knows me," Shemika persisted. "Surely you can get her nanny to come back."

"The woman flew to England," he said helplessly.

"Well, she should be with someone she feels safe with."

"Do you think I don't know that?"

"Did Sadiya have any close girlfriends who could take her?"

"No," he said abruptly. "And I'd prefer not to go there."

"Then what do you want to do?"

"I'll come get her."

"I think that's the best idea."

"Shemika," he warned, "you cannot let her see the newspapers. It's bad."

"I'll make sure."

"I was thinking that maybe next weekend the three of us could go to your mother's house in the Hamptons. You know, get out of the spotlight."

"Not a good plan," she said, imagining Nancy's reaction to that.

"Why not?"

"Uh...we have to talk, Touch. My mother is in a state."

"What kind of state is she in?"

"She wants us to...postpone the wedding."

"Jesus, I hadn't even thought about it, but I suppose in view of the circumstances, we should."

"It seems to be the right thing to do."

"Nancy must be driving you nuts."

"She is," Shemika said, cradling the phone under her chin. "She, uh...she really wants more than that."

"More than what?" Touch asked suspiciously.

"More than a postponement. She thinks I should give you back the ring."

"What?"

"I know it's ridiculous, and I wouldn't even consider it, but that's what she's saying."

"Your mother is a bitch," he said harshly. "And I don't use that word lightly."

"I know."

"What did you tell her when she said this?"

"That there was no way I was breaking up with you."

"Thank God! Because I couldn't go through this without you, Shemika. We both know I'm not the best at expressing my feelings, but believe me, you mean everything to me."

"I never wanted a big wedding anyway," she said, attempting to lighten the conversation. "Did you?"

"We were doing it for her," he acknowledged.

"Absolutely," she agreed.

"Then this could work to our advantage."

"It could?"

"Of course. We can fly off to the Bahamas or somewhere remote and have a simple ceremony."

"I'd like that."

"Okay, sweetie. I'll be there to get Camryn within the hour."

He hung up the phone and wondered what he could do with Camryn to keep her safe and happy. He had things to take care of and, much as he wanted to be with his daughter, now was not the time.

His housekeeper, Mrs. Conner, entered the kitchen. "I'm so sorry for your loss, Mr. Bentley," she said, in a hushed tone, her Scottish burr quite soothing. "I wasn't certain if you'd want me to come in today. If you like, I can—"

"No, no," he said quickly. "I do want you here. I was hoping you could keep Camryn company. I don't think I should send her back to school yet, and I know she enjoys spending time with you. It's difficult, and what with Nanny Reece deserting me…"

"Of course, I'll spend time with the wee girl, Mr. Bentley. Where is the little lassie?"

"She slept over at my fiancée's. I'm on my way to get her now."

"I'll make her those tasty buttermilk pancakes she gobbles up. Not to worry, Mr. Bentley, she'll be happy, and well looked after with me. I raised three wee ones of my own."

"Thank you, Mrs. Conner," he said gratefully.

Krush wandered into the kitchen. "What's going on?" he asked. "I could hear you pacing around all night. Those hardwood floors are a bitch."

"I discovered a few things," Touch said grimly.

"Anything interesting?" Krush asked, pouring himself a glass of orange juice.

"As a matter of fact, yes," Touch said. Glancing at Mrs. Conner, he added, "Why don't you come with me to collect Camryn, and I'll fill you in?"

***

Shemika put down the phone and went to find Camryn. The little girl was sitting in the middle of the bed, sobbing.

"I want my mommy," Camryn cried in a tear-soaked voice. "Where's my mommy?"

"Daddy's coming to get you," Shemika promised, feeling depressed and out of her depth. "He'll be here soon. While we're waiting, why don't you let me help you get dressed?"

"Don't wanna get dressed," Camryn shouted.

With everything that was going on, Shemika did not feel at all equipped to deal with a smart-ass five-year-old, but she was doing her best. "Why not?" she asked patiently.

"Don't have my clothes here," Camryn muttered.

"Yes, you do. You've got the pretty dress you had on yesterday."

"Don't wanna wear that again."

"Why not?"

"I want my mommy!" Camryn yelled.

"I know," Shemika said sympathetically. "And if you get dressed, you'll be all ready for Daddy when he gets here."

"But I want Mommy, not Daddy," Camryn said, lower lip quivering.

"Mommy can't come right now, but Daddy's in his car, and he's racing to get you. I know he'll want to see you all dressed and pretty," she said, handing Camryn her dress.

"Wore that yesterday," Camryn said, flinging the dress back at Shemika. "Want other clothes."

"You don't have any other clothes here."

"Want my jeans," Camryn whined.

"I just told you," Shemika said patiently. "We don't have your clothes here. Daddy will take you to get them." Camryn threw her a furious glare.

"I've got an excellent idea," Shemika said brightly. "Let's go eat breakfast."

"Don't want breakfast," Camryn said, sulking.

"Is there anything you do want?"

"Yes, I want my mommy," Camryn mumbled, her eyes filling with tears. "Where's my mommy?"

Shemika leaned over and attempted to hug her, but Camryn shoved her away. "You know, Camryn," Shemika said softly, refusing to get upset. "Wouldn't it be nice if you and I were friends? We could do fun things together. I could buy you that Hello Kitty stuff you like, and maybe we could take a trip to Disneyland."

"No stupid Disneyland," Camryn said stubbornly. "I want my mommy!"

"Well," Shemika said. "I'll leave your dress here, and if you put it on and come into the kitchen, I'll make us some waffles. How's that?"

"No waffles."

"Okay, I'll be in the kitchen if you change your mind."

With Famous around, it hadn't been so difficult dealing with Camryn. He'd joked and laughed with the little girl, who was obviously fond of him. But as soon as Camryn had fallen asleep watching her movie and he'd carried her into Shemika's bed, Shemika had asked him to leave.

"I thought we could talk now," he'd said.

"This isn't the right time," she replied.

"We have to talk sometime," he'd said, trying to get her to look him in the eye, which she'd refused to do.

"Not now. I'm feeling very fragile. It's been an unbelievable day, and with Camryn here, I can't get into what happened between us."

"So, you're saying you don't want to talk about it?" he'd said, refusing to give up.

"What is there to say?" she'd murmured, shrugging helplessly. "Neither of us knew the consequences of what we did. You obviously didn't know who I was, and I certainly didn't know who you were. I'm embarrassed and kind of...confused. So please go, Famous." Reluctantly he'd left.

After he'd gone, she'd regretted sending him away. And then she'd been overcome with guilt for feeling that way. It wasn't fair to Touch, especially in view of what was going on.

It was quite a situation to find herself in, and now she had her mother on her case, telling her that she had to break up with Touch and go away on a trip. What did the woman think? That she would simply give up her job and take off? It was so typical of Nancy, imagining she was doing the right thing to save the precious family name.

For as long as she could remember, her mother had blackmailed her with the threat of her inheritance from Grandma Poppy, but Grandma Poppy would never cut her off. Her grandma was a kind, generous, and very smart old lady. There was no way she'd listen to Nancy.

Besides, Shemika didn't care whether she inherited the money or not. Life wasn't about how much money you had, and there was no way she was letting Touch down at this time. He was hurting, and so was she.

Eventually, she'd taken a blanket and curled up on the couch, sleeping fitfully.

Now she was in the kitchen toasting frozen waffles for a child who couldn't stand her.

***

On Tuesday morning, Kareema was intent on dragging Famous into the famous photographer Antonio D's studio when all he wanted was to go over to Touch's to see if there was anything he could do to help.

Kareema was having none of it. "They pay you bene money," she announced. "Is it nice, no?"

"Yeah, sure, but—"

"You have a reputation, Famous," Kareema said sternly, all glamorous and business-like in tight-fitting Seven jeans, a Valentino masculine-style jacket, and Jimmy Choo boots. "You cannot bail from job at the last minute. You missed fittings yesterday. Fortunately, I know your body. I found man same size; they do the fittings anyway." Then she decided that she'd better lighten up before he got really pissed. "You'll love the clothes, baby, so sexy," she purred affectionately. "You sexy boy, sì?"

He hated it when she called him 'boy'. She was only five years older than him, so what was with that?

"I shouldn't be doing this gig," he complained, running his hand through his hair. "It doesn't feel right with everything my brother's going through."

"You spent yesterday with him," Kareema pointed out. "Today you work, is not your problem, baby."

"That's cold, Kareema," he said restlessly. "Touch's wife was murdered, and she's not his wife. He was divorced."

"It's still something he has to deal with. Sadiya was Camryn's mother."

"Famous," Kareema said, a touch icy. "I came to New York; we do photos together. Antonio shoots the photos. I insist they use you, so you cannot disappoint."

So, there he was in a cab with Kareema, passing the news-stands where the headlines screamed about the murder. It was all one big stinking mess.

Last night he'd got nowhere with Shemika. She'd be-haved like a nervous racehorse, ready to back off if he so much as touched her arm. He'd finally left because he hadn't wanted to upset her. Was he ever going to get a chance to tell her how he felt? Although he had to agree, the timing was bad.

Kareema had been out when he'd got back to Eddie's apartment the night before. She and Alexia Ciccone had ap-parently hit the town, clubbing until two in the morning. When she'd finally come home and attempted to wake him, he'd pretended to be asleep as she'd tried to work her sexual magic. The problem was that his dick had not been in agree-ment with his mind. Taking advantage, Kareema had climbed aboard and ridden him for a fast five minutes before he came. Then, unfazed, she'd rolled away and finished herself off.

All the while, he'd pretended to be asleep.

Apparently, nothing bothered Kareema. She was a self-contained ball of fire—a girl who took what she wanted whenever it suited her.

For the first time in his life, he'd felt like a piece of meat. Not a pleasant feeling, although he guessed that during his stoned-out-of-his-mind years, he'd left a lot of girls feeling the same way. At least he wasn't that person anymore. Now he was together and caring.

Yeah, so freaking caring that all he could think about was getting back with his brother's fiancée.

Nice. Very nice.

And, hopelessly, he realized there was nothing he could do about it.

Von Diesel

Chapter Four

Red Bentley did not take kindly to being dragged into the headlines.

Sadiya's murder and the subsequent publicity were nothing but an inconvenience. He was livid that his name was being connected to the killing of the Russian floozy Touch had been foolish enough to marry. He'd warned him the first time he'd met Sadiya.

"She's a Russian prostitute," he'd informed his eldest son. "She's marrying you for your money and a green card. That's what those Russian prostitutes do."

"How dare you speak about my future wife like that?" Touch had said. "For your information, she has a green card, and she's a very intelligent and lovely woman with a job. She doesn't need my money."

"You'll learn," Red had muttered. "Just like you learned about that little tramp you took to your prom. Remember her? She couldn't wait for a good fucking from her boyfriend's old man."

"You raped her," Touch accused.

"Is that what you think?" Red had sneered, cracking a nasty smile. "She was begging for it, son. Begging for some hard dick you weren't capable of giving her."

It was the closest Touch had ever come to smashing his father in the face. Instead, he'd stopped speaking to him for several months until Lady J Bentley had intervened. She'd needed some support for one of her charities, so she'd invited Sadiya and Touch to dinner. Why he'd allowed Sadiya to accept still puzzled him, but like his brothers, deep down, he was hoping the old man would change, and they could forge some kind of relationship. How nice it would be to have a father who gave a shit.

Sadiya had loved being in the company of such an important billionaire mogul and his titled girlfriend. She had been all over Red. But Red hadn't changed, he was as appalling as ever, and Touch had hated every minute, refusing to socialize with them again, in spite of Sadiya's pleas.

With the headlines informing New York of Sadiya's brutal murder, Red stomped around his house, yelling at anyone who got in his way. He was furious with Lady J. The bitch had invaded his safe and read his Will. She'd also snooped through his private papers and found out things nobody knew about. Now she was threatening to make certain things public unless he paid out an exorbitant amount of money.

Her lawyer, no slouch in the working-fast department, was requesting a settlement in the neighborhood of thirty-five million dollars. Five million a year for the six years they'd lived together. And this was only the beginning.

"Considering how much you're worth, you're getting off easy," she'd informed him.

Bitch. Whore. They were all whores. They all had a price. And he should know, he'd married enough of them.

***

Touch drove erratically, jamming on the brakes at every red light, causing his Mercedes to jolt to an abrupt stop. He'd dismissed his driver so that he and Krush could talk privately.

"What's going on?" Krush asked, making sure his seatbelt was tightly fastened. "Did you go over to Sadiya's apartment last night?" Touch nodded.

"You got in?"

"No problem."

"And?"

"Sadiya had plenty of secrets. I found the box she kept them locked up in," Touch said, swerving to avoid a jay-walking pedestrian.

"You took the box out of the apartment?"

"I did."

"Which means you removed property that does not belong to you from a crime scene. That's not smart, Touch."

"I did it for my daughter. I have to protect Camryn."

"What did you find?"

"Try half a million bucks in cash."

"Cash. From you?"

"Not from me. Sadiya received a very large divorce settlement, plus the apartment. The only money I pay her is child support, and that goes directly into her bank account."

"Then where's this cash from?" Krush asked.

"Who the fuck knows? And not only cash but several loose gemstones in plastic holders. Bentleys and emeralds, large ones, probably worth a couple of mill. It doesn't make any sense."

"Anything else?"

"This is a good one. It's her original birth certificate. She was ten years older than she claimed, which would make her forty-nine instead of thirty-nine. And a copy of her marriage certificate to Draygo," he said, almost rear-ending a cab. "She certainly took me for a ride. What a lying bitch!"

"She's dead, Touch," Krush reminded him. "There's nothing you can do now."

"I know," Touch said bitterly. "But how could she do this to Camryn?
Everything about her was fraudulent."

"I'm sure she never imagined it would end this way."

"There was also a phone book filled with names I never heard her mention, mostly Russian."

"Could it be from when she lived in Moscow?"

"No, these names are attached to American phone numbers. Sadiya had a secret life nobody knew about. I certainly didn't."

"Have you thought of handing everything over to the detectives and letting them get into it?"

"It's not an option," Touch said, blasting his horn at a blonde in a Volvo, who was intent on cutting him off.

"It's not, huh?" Krush said, bracing his feet against the floor in front of his seat.

"No, Krush. I'm protecting my daughter."

"I don't know what to say, Touch. Are you planning on hunting Draygo down? "Because I never figured you as the vigilante Denzel Washington type."

"I have no idea what I'm going to do. I'm sure if I wait, Draygo will come back with more blackmail threats, and that's the time I'll call in the police or the FBI."

"You know," Krush said thoughtfully. "I'm kind of not getting this. Maybe you can help me out."

"Go ahead."

"You can't tell them what you know now, but if he comes back asking for more money, you can tell them then."

"That's right."

"What's the difference? The headlines will read the same."

"I know. But I need a couple of days to clear my head."

Krush shrugged. Touch was playing a dangerous game, and he didn't want any part of it. "As long as you know what you're doing," he said, thinking how much he didn't want to be here. He'd prefer to be back in L.A. dealing with his house and all his other problems.

"I don't," Touch said, "but I'll figure it out."

***

Antonio was a legend among photographers. He was up there with Richard Avedon, David Bailey, and Helmut Newton. Seventy-five years old, Italian, and crotchety, he greeted Kareema like a long-lost lover, plying her with compliments, words of praise, and suggestive remarks. A diminutive man, small and neat, groomed to perfection, he was very demanding of his many assistants. He only worked when the feeling took him. His early photographs were gallery treasures and sold for thousands of dollars.

Ignoring Famous, he escorted Kareema into the make-up room, raving in Italian about how her beauty blossomed more each year. Naturally, Kareema was in compliment heaven.

"Did you fuck him?" Famous asked as they sat near each other, having their make-up applied.

Kareema gave a secret smile, which signaled a big fat yes.

"You gotta be shitting me," Famous said, throwing her a disgusted look. "He's old enough to be your freaking grandfather."

"I was fifteen," Kareema said coyly. "My first cover for Italian Vogue.

Antonio was so famous and so adorable, I couldn't resist."

"Adorable, my ass," Famous muttered.

"He is brilliant, baby. You will see."

"Yeah, well, all I'm gonna see is the two of you creaming all over each other. Great way to spend the day."

"Jealous?" Kareema inquired, enjoying every minute.

"Are you nuts? Of that old creep?"

"I love it when you get possessive, baby," Kareema purred, her hand reaching over to touch his thigh. "You are so sexy."

He didn't feel sexy; he felt edgy and unsettled. All he could think about was Shemika, and here he was having a conversation with Kareema about being jealous. If she only knew! What a joke.

***

"Daddy!" Camryn shrieked, flinging herself at Touch. "My daddy!"

"What about me?" Krush asked ruefully. "Don't I get a hug too?"

The little girl squealed with laughter, delighted to be the center of attention once more. "Okay, Uncle Krush, give me a hug," she said with a shy smile.

"Have you been a good girl?" Touch asked.

"She's been very good," Shemika assured him.

"Wanna go home," Camryn said, pulling on his sleeve. "Wanna go home now, Daddy."

"We're on our way," Touch said, mouthing a silent thank you to Shemika as she escorted them to the door.

"Did Famous behave himself?" Krush asked. As soon as the words were out of his mouth, he regretted it. Shemika blushed a deep red, and he was aware that she had immediately guessed he knew. Shit! He'd made a big mistake.

"I'll call you later," Touch said, unaware of Shemika's discomfort.

Camryn skipped out of the apartment without so much as a "Thank you." Not that Shemika minded; she was happy to see them leave.

Since when has everything become so complicated?

Oh, yes, since she'd slept with Famous and oh God, Krush obviously knew all about it. The way he'd looked at her after he'd said, "Did Famous behave himself?" It was a dead give-away. How sad was that? Even worse, what if he told Touch?

Unthinkable.

Or was it?

Now she had something else to worry about.

***

Lady J Bentley sat in her bedroom, contemplating her future. Her lawyer had acted swiftly, and that was good. What wasn't good was the information she was burdened with. She knew one too many secrets about Red Bentley, and she'd told him she knew, which she should never have done until she was out of the house.

But it was a Catch 22 situation. If she left, Red would never settle the money on her that she deserved. And after living with Red Bentley for six years, she'd earned every cent.

Of course, thirty-five million was a lot of money. But Red Bentley was worth billions. She was entitled to a worthy pay-out–she'd put in her time.

Her lawyer had told her not to worry. "There's nothing he can do to you," he'd said. "He can't throw you out, so stay where you are and do not leave the house."

Her lawyer didn't have to put up with Red invading her room every so often and screaming abuse. She'd tried locking the door, but that had only made things worse. He'd hammered on it with his steel-tipped cane, roaring obscenities.

Fatima, Mae, the cook, and a couple of the maids had come running to see what was going on. Angrily, he'd waved his stick at them, and they'd fled.

Finally, Lady J had unlocked her door and endured even more verbal abuse.

As long as it was only verbal, she could take it. If it went any further, she was calling the police, and Red would not appreciate that. Especially with all the dreadful publicity about the murder of Touch's ex-wife, a woman to whom Lady J had never warmed.

Sadiya Bentley had been a conniving social-climber, and Russian too. She was classless and, in Lady J's book, there was nothing worse than a classless over-achiever.

***

Running into the photo session late, Shemika was greeted by an ecstatic Nigel standing outside the studio puffing on a cigarette. "Wait until you see them together," he raved, blowing perfect little smoke rings. "Our clothes have never looked so brilliant! The men's line is divine. Chic, simple, and very Italian. And as for Famous, oh, my God!" He paused to take a breath. "Oh dear, sorry. Here I am carrying on about fashion, while you, poor girl—"

"I don't want to talk about it," Shemika said, holding up her hand. "Except to say that we're postponing the wedding, so pass the word."

"No!" Nigel exclaimed in a shocked tone. "How can you?"

"In lieu of what's happened, it's necessary, Nigel. Think about it."

"I suppose you're right," he said, stubbing out his cigarette on the ground.

"But it's such a shame."

"Is the journalist from *People* here?" she asked briskly, determined to get back to work.

"Sassy's dealing with him. We didn't think you'd be in today, let alone come to the photoshoot."

"There's nothing I can do," Shemika said. "I looked after Camryn last night, but now she's back with Touch."

"But surely Touch—"

"I told you, he's with his daughter," she said, walking into the studio. "He's fine, Nigel. You don't have to worry about him."

Then she spotted Famous. He was standing in front of the camera, looking sensational in a lightweight cream-colored sports jacket, a blue striped shirt, and faded jeans. His hair was slightly messed up, his intense blue eyes mesmerizing.

Kareema was draped all over him in an almost transparent white shirt tied under her magnificent breasts, tight white pants, and high-heeled, jeweled sandals. Her auburn hair, piled on top of her head, was a jumble of sexy curls. Nigel was right; they made an amazing-looking couple.

Frank Sinatra's crooning "Come Fly With Me" was blaring over the sound system. Antonio would only work with the voices of Sinatra, Tony Bennett, or Dean Martin. He was an old-time kind of guy.

"Shemika!" Kareema cooed, spotting Shemika and running over to her. "I am so sorry! What a tragedia." She enveloped Shemika in a big warm hug. "You will be bene, no?"

"Thanks, Kareema," Shemika said, exchanging a quick glance with Famous. Were they ever going to get a chance to talk things through? She doubted it.

"Excuse me," Antonio shouted. "We are working here! Kareema, the camera, immediately!"

"The maestro calls," Kareema said, licking her full lips. "Did you see Famous? My sexy boyfriend looks so delizioso. How do you say in America, tasty enough to eat?"

For a moment, Shemika wanted to scream, just let loose and yell her lungs out. But what good would that do?

Everyone would think she was crazy, and she still had a job to take care of. Fixing a smile on her face, she approached Sassy and the journalist from *People*. It was time to stop thinking about herself and get back to work.

Chapter Five

"I was hoping we could talk before you read about Mrs. Bentley's murder in the newspapers," Fatima said over the phone. "I left several messages. Why didn't you call me back before?"

"I'm sorry," Velvet said. "I only just saw a copy of the New York Post."

"As terrible as it is, it hasn't really affected us at the house," Fatima continued. "Touch Bentley was divorced from her, although Red Bentley is quite upset about all the publicity."

Who cares whether Red Bentley is upset? Velvet thought. I certainly don't.

"I'm in L.A.," she blurted.

"Excuse me?" Fatima responded.

"I've been booked on a modeling assignment."

"You flew to L.A. without telling me?"

"It happened suddenly."

"What happened suddenly?"

"My friend Chanel introduced me to a modeling agent," she explained. "He sent me out on an interview, and I got the job. Exciting, isn't it?"

Obviously, Fatima did not think it was exciting at all. "You're only nineteen, inexperienced," she said, sounding worried. "What makes you think the people you're working for are legitimate? They could be white slaving you. That kind of thing still goes on, you know."

"You've been watching too much CSI on TV, Mama," Velvet said. "Anyway, in my case, it would be black slaving, wouldn't it?"

"It's true, Velvet," Fatima said, ignoring her daughter's sarcasm. "Do you know anything at all about the people who took you there?"

"Nobody took me here," Velvet said. "The modeling agency is very reputable. I'm staying in a great hotel by the beach, and they're treating me like a princess. Plus, I'm working with a well-known photographer who's shooting me for the cover of a new magazine."

"This is all moving too fast for me." Fatima sighed. "One day you want to be a singer, the next you're a model."

"I still want to sing, Mama," Velvet said softly. "You know that's always been my ambition. But this job pays a lot of money. I couldn't turn it down, and I'm glad I didn't."

"Everything isn't always about money," Fatima said.

"Really?" Velvet responded. "Wasn't that why you went to work for Mr. Bentley, 'cause you needed the money?"

"That was different."

"Okay, Mama," Velvet said, anxious to get off the phone. "Why don't I tell you all about it when I get home? I'll even treat you to a big fancy dinner."

"How's that?"

"When will you be back?"

"Thursday night."

"Velvet," Fatima said hesitantly, "the two of us...we need to sit down and have a conversation."

"About what?" Velvet asked, wondering if Fatima had heard that Malshonda had moved out, and now she was preparing to give her a lecture on the dangers of a young girl living alone in New York.

"The things I told you about your father, well...I wasn't quite truthful with you."

"Huh?"

"There's something else you should know."

"What?" she asked sharply.

"Not over the phone."

"Mama," she sighed, "for God's sake, why are you playing with my emotions like this?"

"When I explain it to you, you'll understand."

"Will I, Mama?" she said, shaking her head. "Will I?" Upset and confused, she walked back to the lunch table and handed Holliday his phone. Just when she'd thought she had answers, Fatima had to come up with this.

She wished she hadn't phoned her mom back; it had ruined her day. And where was Malshonda when she needed her? They'd always talked about everything, and now she had nobody to share things with, good or bad.

The "team" whisked her off for more changes: a different hairstyle, make-up touch-ups, an incredibly sexy one-piece red swimsuit with strategic cut-outs.

Once they were back on the beach, Holliday, who was a real sweetheart, asked her if everything was alright.

"Why?" she asked apprehensively. "Am I not looking okay?"

"You're coming across in the pics as a tad uptight."

"Oh, God, I'm sorry. It's my mom," she confessed. "She's impossible to understand."

"Ah," Holliday said wisely. "If we understood our parents, the world would be a much calmer place."

"Right," Velvet agreed.

Making a concentrated effort, she put the conversation with Fatima out of her head and once more threw herself into posing.

At six o'clock, Savage announced they were through for the day. "I'm inviting everyone for dinner," he said, a crooked grin going full force. "Ivy at the Shore. Seven-thirty in the lobby."

"What's Ivy at the Shore?" Velvet asked Uma, the stylist, as they walked towards the hotel.

"A restaurant," Uma replied, giving her a look as if to say, what rock have you been hiding under?

"Uh...I don't have anything to wear," Velvet said, frowning.

"This is L.A.," Holliday said. "Nobody dresses up here unless it's a big event or you're Paris Hilton."

"Jeans will do," Quinn added. "It's casual."

They all headed into the lobby of Shutters. As they started towards the elevator, a male voice called out, "Velvet?"

"Oh my God!" Quinn exclaimed in a stage whisper. "It's Tony A. Do you know him?"

Velvet stopped and stared as a handsome young man dressed all in white rushed towards them, trailed by what appeared to be his team.

"Tony?" she questioned excitedly. "Is that you?"

"Velvet? I don't believe it!" he yelled, hugging her, then standing back.

"Look at you! You're a glamour queen."

"You're the queen," Quinn muttered under his breath.

"Shut up!" Holliday hissed. "Velvet actually knows him!"

"Who's Tony A?" Uma asked as they all watched Velvet and Tony embrace.

"Only the hottest Latino singer since Ricky Martin wowed them at the Grammys," Holliday said, rubbing his hands together.

"Gay playing it straight," Quinn said. "But I have to admit, gorgeous all the same."

"This is amazing!" Tony said, shaking his head in admiration as he checked Velvet out. "What are you doing here?"

"Shooting a cover for a magazine."

"You're a model?" he said, flashing whiter than white teeth in a dazzling smile.

"And you're Tony A," she responded. "Wow! I've listened to your song on the radio. I never put it together that it was you."

Tony Artura, the Puerto Rican boy who used to live next door to her in Harlem until Fatima had yanked her away to Manhattan and the Bentley mansion, was standing in front of her. The boy who'd taken her rollerblading in Central Park, taught her to pick at a guitar and helped her with her homework. And then, when she'd moved back to live with Aunt Aretha and Malshonda, he was the boy she'd been serious with until his mom had decided they were moving to Miami.

Tony Artura, her first big crush. Now he was Tony A, the new Latino singing sensation with a big hit record. What a rush!

"You know," he said, still smiling, "I often thought about you, wondered how you were doing."

"Then how come you didn't phone or write?"

He shrugged. "Things changed when we moved out of New York. I got into a performing-arts school that kept me really busy. It was all work, work, work. My mom had big ambitions for me."

"You look great," Velvet said, reaching out to touch his low-Caesar haircut.

"So do you. I always knew you'd turn out to be a beauty."

"Thanks."

"You were such a skinny little runt with those long spider legs and wild green eyes."

"And you had an S-Curl!" she teased. "Guess you want to forget about that."

They both started laughing. "How about we get together later for a drink?" Tony suggested. "Catch up on everything."

43

"What time?"

"I'm performing at a charity event in Beverly Hills. I should be back around eleven."

"Call me," she said, hoping he would. "If I'm still awake, I'd love to." A dark-haired, slim-hipped Hispanic man inserted himself between them. "Aren't you going to introduce me to your friend?" he said to Tony, arching his finely plucked eyebrows.

"Yeah, sure," Tony replied, a touch awkwardly. "Hector, this is Velvet."

"Hello…Velvet," Hector said, giving her a full-on dirty look.

"Velvet and I went to school together," Tony explained, "and we lived next door to each other."

"Back in the day," Velvet said, smiling.

"We have to go," Hector continued. "We cannot be late."

"Well," Velvet said wistfully, "it was great seeing you, Tony. Your success is fantastic."

"You too, my little Velvet. Sooo beautiful."

"Come on," Hector said, impatiently tapping his watch. "The limo is waiting."

"I guess the limo is waiting," Velvet said, still smiling.

"I guess it is," Tony responded, smiling back.

"Bye for now. Don't forget, I'll call you later."

Impulsively she leaned forward and kissed his cheek. "Thanks for all the fun memories," she whispered. "You made growing up kind of special."

Before she could say anything else, Hector successfully dragged him away.

Holliday was in a state of excitement. "You know Tony A," he said, his voice filled with admiration. "You actually know him."

"Obviously, she does," Uma said drily, herding them all into the elevator.

"Then, if you know him so well," Quinn said, "you should advise him to haul his sexy little butt out of the closet. His gay fans are not pleased he's pretending to be straight. Who exactly does he think he's fooling?"

"He wasn't gay when I knew him," Velvet said.

"He certainly is now," Quinn replied crisply. "He's the talk of the gay community."

"He is?"

"Everyone knows. And that was the boyfriend."

"What makes you think he's got a boyfriend?" Velvet asked, remembering the fun she and Tony had shared, fooling around without actually going all the way. She'd been a very young teenager at the time, but she recalled that Tony had been a fantastic kisser, almost on a par with Tristin. And he'd never objected to the many blowjobs she'd put his way. Ah...fond memories...

"Because it's obvious," Quinn snapped. "That guy was in full drool mode over Tony, and he hated you."

"He did?"

"Hated you. If Tony had stayed any longer, Hector would've thrown a jealous fit! Do not expect a phone call later. Hector will not allow it." The elevator ground to a halt at her floor, and she got off.

"See you in the lobby at seven-thirty," Holliday called after her. "Don't forget, very casual."

Sure. Like she had anything that wasn't casual. She hadn't possessed a dress since she was twelve.

So, she thought, Tony Artura is Tony A. If it can happen for him...

She opened the door to her room and was amazed to find it filled with orchids. White orchids, lilac orchids, pink orchids, exotic and beautiful baskets dominated every surface space.

A white card was propped up against the biggest arrangement. She opened the card and read the message:

Orchids stun my senses.

So do you, LL.

It was Tristin. Nobody else called her LL.

She experienced a shiver of excitement. As if the orchids weren't enough, five minutes later, he was on the phone.

"Thanks for the beautiful orchids," she said. "How am I supposed to get them back to New York?"

"On the plane," he said casually.

"I won't be able to carry them; there are too many. Besides, I don't think airlines allow—"

"My plane," he interrupted.

"Your plane," she said disbelievingly.

"That's right."

"You've got a plane?"

"The company does. I call it mine because I own the company."

"Tristin—"

"I like it when you use my name. You got a sexy voice, LL. You know that?"

"You're crazy."

"No, you're the crazy one," he insisted. "Running out on me when I was all set to hook you up with the right producer. Weren't you the girl who was ragging on me to get her a singing career?"

"I still want it," she said, delighted to hear his voice. "It was just that this modeling thing came along, and I really need the money, so I couldn't say no."

"Hey, I was under the impression you were an expert at saying no."

"Excuse me?"

"You've managed to say it to me a few times."

"That's different."

"It is? Explain to me how."

"If I have to mention that you're married one more time—"

"Are you dressed?" he interrupted.

"What?"

"Dressed? Clothes on?"

"Why?"

"Cause there's someone at your door."

"No, there's not."

And, sure enough, there was a knock on the door.

"Who is it?" she called out.

"Room Service."

"Hang on," she said to Tristin, thinking, *what now?*

She opened the door expecting more orchids because over-the-top seemed to be Tristin's style.

What she didn't expect was Tristin himself. Handsome, cool, killer grin, black pants, and a black shirt. Bentley studs in his ears, extravagant Bentley watch, along with his cell phone in hand. Behind him stood another man, bigger and blacker, dressed in a casual maroon outfit.

"LL," Tristin said. "Meet Parker J. Jones. He's gonna be your producer."

Von Diesel

Chapter Six

Sometime in the middle of a break during the Ciccone photoshoot, Famous managed to corner Shemika and insist they get together later to talk things through. "Tonight," he said, sounding like he meant business.

"I can't," she demurred, wishing she could stop dissolving into a shivering wreck every time he was close to her.

"Why not?" he demanded.

"Because we've, uh, had to postpone the wedding. My mother wants me over at her house to check through lists and make sure everyone is covered."

"Hey," he said, fixing her with his almond-colored eyes, "aren't you and I talking more important than that?"

"And then I might have to see Touch," she added, although she already knew she wasn't seeing him that night.

"Shemika, Shemika," Famous said, shaking his head. "Stop fighting the inevitable. I'll come to your apartment. It's the only place we can be private. Just tell me what time, and I'll be there."

"No, not my apartment," she said quickly.

"Why not?" he asked, glancing around to make sure Kareema wasn't nearby.

Why not? Good question. Could it be because she didn't trust herself to be alone with him?

No. Absolutely not. He was a one-night fling, her future brother-in-law, and nothing like that would ever happen again.

"Okay," she said, agreeing reluctantly. "Seven o'clock."

"I'll be there."

"Where will you be, baby?" Kareema asked sweetly, appearing out of nowhere, flinging an arm around Famous's shoulders.

He didn't take a beat. "Shemika was arranging a surprise for Touch. I'm helping her out."

"Surprise?" Kareema cooed, stroking his cheek.

"It wouldn't be a surprise if we told everyone, would it?" he said, edging away from her.

Shemika remembered his words from the day before, *"Kareema and I, we're not a couple."*

Well, they sure looked like a couple. And Kareema was living in his apartment. So, what did that make them? Oh, yes. A couple!

Not that she cared. Why should she?

And yet, somehow, she did.

As each day passed, she was becoming more and more confused. If only Famous hadn't reappeared in her life, she would probably have been able to forget all about him, but no. That hadn't happened. He was everywhere.

Later, as the photoshoot wound down, Nigel cornered her. "Feel like going for a drink?" he asked. "An apple martini would slide down very nicely."

"I can't," Shemika responded. "I'm meeting my mother. We're going over cancellation lists and stuff."

"Poor you," Nigel commiserated. "Nancy must be driving you insane. I know how anal she can be."

"Hmm…" Shemika answered, thinking what an astute liar she was becoming.

"I stole a couple of pics," Nigel confessed, lowering his voice like a naughty schoolboy. "Aren't I the bad one?"

"You did?" she murmured, her mind elsewhere.

"Antonio does not allow his pics to leave his studio, but I fail to see why we shouldn't have some. Here," he said, handing her a photo, "one for you."

She glanced at the photo. Naturally, it was of Famous looking unbelievably handsome with Kareema behind him.

Her arms draped lovingly around his neck. "What am I supposed to do with it?" she asked blankly.

"I thought you'd like to have it," Nigel said. "Stick it on your screen saver and enjoy the view."

"I'm sure Touch would be pleased about that," she said tartly.

"Isn't it a coincidence," Nigel mused, "that this hot male model should turn out to be your fiancé's brother? He's your family too, or at least he soon will be. Can you imagine Christmas and Thanksgiving and all the holidays you'll spend together? He and Kareema will have beautiful babies. You and Touch will too. You'll be such a gorgeous family, straight out of an *Empire* ad."

"Stop thinking ahead, Nigel," she said, wishing he'd shut up.

"Oh, sorry," Nigel said apologetically. "I keep on forgetting what you're going through. Postponing the wedding must be getting you down."

"It is."

"I understand perfectly," Nigel said, giving her a sympathetic pat on the shoulder. "Please give Touch my best regards and tell him I'm so sorry about everything."

"I'll do that," she said, heading out of the door.

She had no intention of seeing her mother or Touch. Her plan was to rush home, take a shower, get herself together, and be ready for Famous at seven o'clock.

Suddenly, she was radiating excitement.

***

Across the studio, Famous watched as Shemika left. This had been one of the most uncomfortable days he could remember. He was standing in front of the camera attempting to look edgy and macho, with Shemika somewhere behind the lights watching him while Kareema draped herself all over him. It was pure torture.

And, to make it even worse, he couldn't stand Antonio. The fussy little photographer was getting on his nerves the way he was constantly kissing up to Kareema.

Halfway through the afternoon, Alexia Ciccone had appeared, dragging with her a young Italian guy who had done nothing but lounge around throwing Famous disgusted looks.

"Did I happen to take his job?" Famous asked Kareema between set-ups.

"No, baby," she purred. "It's simply that Alexia is so competitive. She thinks if you can be a model, why can't Carlo? She doesn't understand that you are a professional."

"Great," Famous said.

"They pay us a lot of money. You no worry."

"Who's worried?" he said irritably.

"Good, because tonight we have dinner with them."

"Can't do that. I have to see Touch," he said quickly, thinking of his meeting with Shemika. Besides, there was nothing he'd like less than dinner with Alexia Ciccone and her jealous boyfriend.

"Really," Kareema said unconcernedly. "Then you will join us later."

"Sure," he agreed, with no intention of doing so.

It occurred to him that it was about time he told Kareema they were over, that he wasn't coming back to Italy, that he didn't want to live with her anymore, that she wasn't his girlfriend, and she should go ahead and find some other guy.

But what if Shemika didn't want anything more to do with him? What if she was in love with Touch, and he'd been no more than a casual one-nighter? Did he really want to leave himself with no options?

Man, it was some situation. He'd never felt this way about anyone before, and it wasn't because Shemika belonged to someone else. It was because he genuinely cared about her.

The bitter truth was that he'd fallen in love with Shemika long before he'd realized she was taken.

***

After a busy day finalizing things with the Japanese bankers, meeting with his executives, visiting the building site, and making sure Camryn was happy with Mrs. Conner, who had agreed to stay over for the rest of the week until he hired a new nanny, Touch had an early steak dinner with Krush, and then met with Detective Banks who had requested another meeting.

Before he'd got together with the detective, Touch had checked with his lawyer, Elliott Minor, who assured him it was just as well to cooperate.

"Why?" he'd asked.

"Because if you don't," Elliott had answered patiently, "it looks as if you've got something to hide."

"Well, I don't."

"I know that. So do they."

"Then why, Elliott?"

"Because it's not about you, Touch. It's about them finding out more about Sadiya."

"What's to find out?" he'd asked guardedly.

"How should I know? Friends, family, you might have answers they haven't come up with. Did she have a boyfriend, for instance? They're investigating a murder, Touch, and a very high-profile one at that. Look, if it makes you more comfortable, I can be there."

"That's not necessary," he said, thinking if he couldn't handle Detective Banks, he was certainly in a sorry state. Besides, he had nothing to hide. Only the fact that he'd taken Sadiya's box from her apartment, which contained more than a few things she obviously hadn't wanted anybody to know about.

Detective Banks turned up on time. As far as Touch was concerned, the man was as annoying as ever, with his cheap aftershave and joke of a mustache.

"Mr. Bentley," Detective Banks said, proffering his clammy hand. "I'm sorry to bother you again. Is it alright if my colleague and I come in and I ask you a few more questions?"

"Certainly," Touch said, leading them into the living room.

Detective Banks' colleague was a broad-faced, overly tall woman with stringy brown hair and a dominating red lipstick that complimented her rather large mouth. She was the same detective who'd spoken to Camryn the day before.

"Good evening, Mr. Bentley," she said in a barely-there voice. "Excuse the way I sound, but I think I'm coming down with something." Nice! A detective breathing germs all over him.

"Can I fix you a drink, Detectives?" Touch asked, pouring himself a brandy.

"Not allowed to drink on duty," Detective Banks said, sitting down on the couch. "But I wouldn't say no to a Seven-Up."

"Let me see," Touch said, checking out the small fridge behind the bar, "how about Diet Coke?"

"Too sweet for me," Detective Banks responded. "I'll take a bottle of water if you've got it."

"Anything for you?" Touch asked the female detective.

She shook her head.

Touch handed Detective Banks a bottle of Evian and sat down on the other couch, facing them.

"I expect you're wondering what we've found out," Detective Banks said, rolling the Evian bottle between his large hands. "I would've thought we might've heard from you."

"Why would you hear from me?" Touch asked.

"Usually, when there's a murder in the family, the relatives are anxious to get an update on any information they can."

"It's been less than forty-eight hours," Touch pointed out. "I presume that when you discover who did this, you'll let me know."

"That's if you don't read about it first," Detective Banks said, stroking his mustache. "I see the press are all over this. I didn't realize your family was so powerful and important."

Was the detective being sarcastic? Touch couldn't tell. He decided to give him the benefit of the doubt. "How can I help you?" he said, hoping to make this a short meeting.

"Were you by any chance in your wife's apartment last night?" Detective Banks asked, producing his weathered notebook and the usual stubby pencil.

This was a tricky one and quite unexpected. Touch couldn't decide whether to lie or tell the truth. Since lying didn't seem like such a clever idea, he answered truthfully. "As a matter of fact, I was," he said casually. "I stopped by to pick up some clothes and a few toys for my little girl. She was very upset, as you can imagine, a child of her age discovering her mother's body. She doesn't realize her mommy is dead. We've told her that she's in the hospital, but it's still very traumatic, and I felt that Camryn needed her things around her."

Von Diesel

"You crossed a police line," Detective Banks said, pursing his lips disapprovingly.

"I didn't think it would matter," Touch replied. "It was my home once, you know. I lived there."

"That was when you were married to Mrs. Bentley, I presume," Detective Banks said, jotting something in his notebook. "However, it's not your residence now, is it?"

"I own the building," Touch couldn't help saying.

"Yes, Mr. Bentley, only I'm sure you understand that there are rules, strict reasons why we secure a crime scene. It's so that people can't go in and tamper with evidence."

"I didn't touch anything," Touch said, trying not to stare at the detective's crooked front teeth. "I went straight to my daughter's room, collected her things, and left."

"I see," Detective Banks said, putting down his notebook and undoing the cap on the bottle of water he'd been hanging on to. "Well, I'm sure you'll be glad to know that your alibi checks out."

"My alibi?"

"The rehearsal dinner."

"Why wouldn't it?" Touch said, his temper rising.

The female detective began to cough.

"You were where you said you were," Detective Banks continued, ignoring both Touch's obvious irritation and his colleague's coughing fit. "But Irena, who we just found out is Mrs. Bentley's mother—"

Touch almost choked on his drink. "Excuse me?" he said. "Irena, Sadiya's personal maid?"

"Yes, we checked things out, and it's clear she is Mrs. Bentley's mother. Although, for some obscure reason, she's not exactly admitting it."

The female detective, still coughing, stood up and requested the bathroom. "By the front door," Touch said, more

56

interested in finding out what else Detective Banks had to say. "What do you mean, she's not admitting it?"

"It always strikes me as strange the way people act when there's been a murder," Detective Banks mused. "It's almost as though everyone has something to hide, and sometimes they do."

"Surely you can't suspect Irena of murdering Sadiya?"

"No, not at all. In fact, it was Irena who informed us that Mrs. Bentley had many friends in the Russian community. Did you know that Mr. Bentley?"

"No, I didn't," he said, thinking of the book he'd found filled with names he'd never heard of.

"Irena seems to think there's a phone book missing," Detective Banks said.

Touch stared at the man. Was he by chance a thought-reader in his spare time?

"It contains the names and numbers of Mrs. Bentley's Russian acquaintances," Detective Banks continued. "Problem is, I can't seem to find it in the apartment. You didn't happen to notice it when you broke in, did you?"

"I didn't break-in," Touch said, resenting the detective's attitude. "I thought I explained it to you. I own the building. I lived in the apartment. I didn't think there was anything wrong with collecting some of my child's personal possessions."

"Right." A long, silent beat. "Please make sure it doesn't happen again, Mr. Bentley."

"What else can I do for you?" Touch asked, standing up in the hope it would indicate their meeting was over.

"I was wondering if you've thought of anything at all that might help us."

"Regarding what?"

"Mrs. Bentley's Russian connections."

"I just told you. I know nothing about them."

"I have a strong hunch it's an inside job," Detective Banks said, peering intently at Touch. "No sign of forced entry, and the robbery was slapdash. It was almost as though the perpetrator murdered the woman, then decided he or she better make it look like a robbery. This crime was committed by someone she knew."

"Really?" Touch said, refilling his brandy glass.

"Yes. I'm almost positive she knew her killer."

"That's interesting," Touch said, returning to the couch.

"I'm wondering if you have any ideas?"

"No," Touch said boldly, anxious to be rid of the man. "We've been divorced for over a year. Sadiya had her own life. I do know she had many acquaintances in New York society, but if she was close to anybody, in particular, I didn't know about it."

"Hmm…" Detective Banks said, picking up his notebook again. "Oh, yes, remind me," he added, chewing on the pencil stub. "Did you say you were unaware that Irena was related to your ex-wife?"

"I was completely unaware of it."

The female detective returned to the room and sat down. She was no longer coughing. Touch found it unnerving that she'd hardly said anything. "Have you spoken to Irena since the murder?" Detective Banks inquired, scribbling something else.

"No, I haven't," Touch snapped. He'd had enough and was anxious for them to leave.

"You might want to."

"Why would I?"

"If Mrs. Bentley was her daughter, then that makes Camryn her granddaughter, doesn't it?"

"I suppose so," Touch said, reluctant to give that thought any credit.

"Irena is carrying on about missing money. It seems Mrs. Bentley was her sole means of support. Apparently, she paid her in cash every week. Irena says there was a stash of cash in the apartment." A short silence. "We can't locate it," Detective Banks said in an almost accusatory tone. "Strange, don't you think?"

"Not at all," Touch answered smoothly. "You said it was a robbery. Obviously, if there was cash lying around, the burglar or burglars took it."

"Hmm...maybe." A beat. "Irena never lived in, did she?"

"No. I think she came three times a week to take care of Sadiya's clothes and personal items."

"Did she have a key?"

"Surely you've asked her?"

"Just double-checking," Detective Banks said, finally standing up.

Touch stood also.

"Um, by the way, was Irena working for your ex-wife when you first got married?"

"No," Touch said, tired of the questions. "Sadiya brought her in a year after that. I was under the impression that she'd hired her from an employment agency."

"I can't think of anything else for now. Can you?" the detective said, glancing over at his colleague.

The female detective shook her head.

Detective Banks moved towards the door. "We'll be in touch," he promised.

Touch walked behind him.

"Oh," the detective said, stopping for a moment. "And you're sure you didn't happen to notice that phone book lying around?"

"I'm positive," Touch said.

"Good night, Mr. Bentley."

"Good night, Detective."

***

While Touch met with the detectives, Krush shut himself in the guest room and started making numerous phone calls, attempting to catch up. One of the first was to Patrick Sumter to check that Patrick's people were handling all the proper preparations for Chilly's upcoming Vegas wedding.

"Don't worry 'bout it," Patrick said in his raspy voice. "Worry 'bout paying me my fucking money."

"Red sends you his best regards," Krush said evenly. "We both enjoyed the joke. You should've been an actor; you missed your calling."

"What fucking joke?"

"The putting on the pressure and the hooker. By the way, I think I told you that she stole my Rolex. Next time hire a better class of girl. Thieving doesn't reflect well on you."

"Shit!" Patrick growled.

"Yeah, shit," Krush agreed. "When I fly in for the wedding, I'll have your money."

He hung up, feeling satisfied. Screw Patrick Sumter. He'd thought they were friends, but one word from Red and it was over.

At least something positive had come out of it. The experience had definitely cured him of gambling fever.

Next, he called Famous. He'd spoken to him earlier and invited him for dinner with Touch, but Famous had explained that he and Kareema had to get together with Alexia Ciccone and her boyfriend. Krush hoped his baby brother wasn't bullshitting him. It wouldn't be cool if he was sniffing around after Shemika. Although, according to Touch, Shemika was spending the evening with her mother.

There was no answer from Famous's cell, so Krush called Chilly, who was in a sweet-as-apple-pie mood, all giggly and girly and full of Las Vegas wedding plans.

"Brewsky's flying to Vegas a few days earlier," she revealed. "Some of his guys are throwing him a bachelor's retreat. Isn't that like, the coolest?"

"What's a bachelor retreat?" Krush asked, inwardly groaning because he knew it would turn out to be trouble.

"You know, the guys sit around, play cards, run movies, hit a few balls, take a boat out on Lake Mead."

Translation: The guys go to Vegas, get totally blasted on tequila shooters, and visit every strip club in town.

"Are you happy about him doing that?" Krush asked.

"Course," Chilly trilled. "My girls are booking us a bungalow at the Beverly Hills Hotel, and we're going to have mani-pedis, facials, mud baths, all kinds of girly stuff."

Translation: The girls sit out by the pool at the Beverly Hills Hotel, downing cosmopolitans and bitching endlessly about their boyfriends.

"Sounds great," Krush lied.

"I know!" Chilly said enthusiastically. "I'm flying back to L.A. tomorrow. You should come with me. My record company is sending me a plane."

"Is Brewsky on it?"

"No. He's gotta see some family, and then he'll go directly to Vegas."

Why not fly with Chilly? Krush thought. He couldn't stay away forever, and Touch seemed intent on doing his own thing.

He'd spoken to Chi-rone several times. The rain had finally stopped, and Chi-rone informed him that he'd managed to salvage quite a lot from his house, including his safe. He had arranged for everything to be cleaned and put in storage, except the safe, which he'd had transported to his own apartment for safekeeping.

Fortunately, the house itself had not slid down the hillside. That was a major bonus.

Chi-rone was a smart kid: he'd already hired architectural contractors to see what could be done about securing the foundations and repairing the damage. A big fat raise was definitely in his future.

Yes, Krush decided, there were many reasons he should get back. "What time are you taking off?" he asked Chilly.

"Around noon," she chirped. "Please come."

"I'll meet you at the airport," he said.

He'd tell Touch about his plans later. He was sure his brother would understand.

Chapter Seven

The Soviet Club was a home away from home for the many Russian expatriates who had made New York their place of residence. The food was good, the vodka the finest, and the atmosphere reminiscent of a fancy European nightspot.

Isha Parker always enjoyed spending time at the Soviet Club. She felt comfortable there. It was light years away from her real-life of girl-on-girl shows and sleeping with rich old men for money. At the Soviet Club, she was regarded as a beautiful woman who loved to enjoy herself. Most people thought she was a beauty consultant, and sometimes if she liked a man she met there, she would sleep with him for free.

Her cousin, Igor, when he bothered to dress properly, was quite a handsome escort in spite of his tendency to put on weight. Draygo, Igor's friend, always managed to look shabby. Although tonight, he, too, had made quite an effort. Isha knew it was on account of Inka. The poor man lusted after Inka, who usually chose to ignore him. Tonight, something was different. Tonight, Draygo had acquired a certain energy that he did not usually possess.

Inka, dazzling in a purple cocktail dress, noticed it too. Swilling back her second White Russian, she hiccupped delicately and said to Isha, "What is with Draygo? You notice a change?"

"Yes," Isha agreed, resplendent in a clinging yellow jersey dress, her new pearls fastened proudly round her neck. "Igor says he has something to tell us." Lowering her voice, Isha added, "Igor says he is getting plenty of money."

"No!" Inka said. "Not Draygo."

"Yes," Isha insisted. "Igor is sure."

There was a noisy group at the next table. There were three very young American girls with two older Russian men.

Isha knew one of the guys, Alex Pinchinoff, a man to steer clear of. Russian Mafia. Dangerous. She'd slept with him once, and that was enough. He'd handcuffed her to his bed and practically choked her to death with his enormous member. She felt sorry for the three young girls sitting at his table. One was going to get very unlucky indeed.

After a hearty meal of steak, potatoes, green beans, and a side salad, Draygo said he had an announcement to make.

Isha downed her third shot glass of vodka and gave him a challenging look. "Go ahead," she said. "Surprise us."

"I will!" Draygo said boldly, shooting an admiring glance at Inka. "I surprise you good."

Inka leaned a little closer to him, her large breasts almost popping out of her purple dress. "Go ahead," she murmured, wondering how he'd be in bed. Plain men were usually better at sex than handsome ones. Inka enjoyed a man who could make her come. Her clients never did, hard as some of them tried.

"My wife," he said, slurring his words. "She die."

"Wife?" Inka said scornfully. "You not have wife. Who would marry you?"

"Go on, tell them," Igor encouraged, his eyes bulging.

"Famous woman, my wife," Draygo boasted. "Famous and rich."

"Lauren London," Inka teased.

"Taraji P. Henson," Isha said, joining in the fun.

"Angela Bassett. She's very sexy," Inka said, licking her lips. "Good for me, not you."

"Draygo is not shitting with you," Igor said, defending his friend. "Draygo was married to woman in newspapers. Murder victim. Famous murder victim. And rich."

"Yes, rich," Draygo agreed. "And she was my wife. I am the legal husband, so all the money is mine."

"No!" Inka said, laughing derisively. "You make up story."

"Show them the document," Igor urged, giving Draygo a sharp nudge. "Show it to them. Then the bitches will believe you."

"Who you calling bitches?" Isha objected while Draygo dug into his pocket and came up with a crumpled marriage certificate. He handed it to Isha.

"Who's Paulina Kuchinova?" Isha said, studying it. "Never heard of her."

"Sadiya Bentley, the society woman who got herself murdered," Draygo said.

Now Isha burst out laughing. "You're full of shit."

"I can prove it."

"How?"

"I have wedding picture that tell story. She was prostitute, like you."

"I not prostitute," Isha said angrily. "I am therapist to very rich men. Prostitutes work the street. They are dirty girls."

"You not a dirty girl?" Draygo said slyly.

"Show me a picture, or you are nothing but lying scum," Isha said, picking up the bottle of vodka from the table and pouring herself another shot.

"I got a picture to show you," Draygo said.

"Then what?" Inka asked, curious as to why he would invent such a story. "You go to the police and tell them she's your wife?"

"After they catch the murderer, yes."

"How do you know they caught him?" Isha asked with a sly wink. "Maybe they think it's you. Maybe they will arrest you."

"Me?" Draygo said, outraged. "I do lot of bad things, but not murder."

"Yeah," Isha said, beginning to feel horny and not believing Draygo's pathetic story. She glanced over at the gangster sitting at the next table.

Alex Pinchinoff caught her eye and raised his glass to her. Apparently, he'd enjoyed a better time than she had during their previous encounter in bed.

Maybe she should give him a second chance, after all. There were no other likely prospects in sight.

*****

"Hi," Shemika said, pulling open her front door.

"Hey," Famous responded, stepping inside. "For you," he said, thrusting a bunch of yellow roses at her.

Why had he bought her flowers? It was a romantic gesture he should not be making. And yet, who was she kidding? It was a sweet thing for him to do. "How are you?" she asked, in her best polite voice.

Dumb question because she'd only left the photoshoot an hour ago, and he'd been fine then.

"Okay," he said, wandering into her living room.

"Uh...would you like a glass of wine?" she asked, feeling awkward as she followed him, clutching the roses, which were beginning to drip.

"I don't drink," he said, realizing how little they knew about each other. Should he confess that he was once a raging alcoholic? A stoned-out-of-his-mind, sex-crazed, drugs-and-booze junkie? Or should he wait and let her discover his nefarious past for herself?

The diplomatic move was to wait. But what the hell? He was determined to be up-front about everything. "I'm in the drug abuse program," he blurted.

"Oh, uh...sorry," she said, taking the flowers into her small kitchen and searching for a vase.

"Sorry that I'm in the program? Or that I don't drink?" he asked, walking in behind her.

"I'm not big on drinking," she said, finding a vase and filling it with water.

"You could've fooled me," he said lightly. "The other night, you were certainly feeling no pain."

Just like that, he was bringing it up. Now it was up to her to defend herself and her actions. "Yes," she admitted, trying not to get uptight. "I was drunk, and I guess that's why I did what I did."

"You weren't that wasted," he said, leaning on the countertop, watching her as she arranged the flowers.

"Yes, I was," she said, trying not to look at him.

"Does this mean that every time you have too much to drink, you fall into bed with a stranger?" he asked, gently teasing her. "Is that what I'm getting here?"

"No. But—"

"Tell me, Shemika," he said, becoming serious, "I gotta know, what happened between us?"

"I...I don't know," she managed, thinking, I'm not ready for a confrontation.

"It's kinda obvious you're not sleeping with Touch." She didn't answer.

A long beat. "Do you love him?"

"It's, it's none of your business," she said, picking up the vase and carrying it into the living room.

"Well, that's a resounding no," he said, once more right behind her.

"Do not put words into my mouth."

"I'm not."

"Yes, you are," she said crossly. "Touch, and I are very happy together."

"So that's why you slept with me. Now I understand, it's 'cause you're so wildly happy with him."

"You know what, Famous?" she said agitatedly. "Meeting like this was a mistake. We have nothing to say to each other, and I don't care to fight. What happened? Well, it just happened. We should leave it at that."

"What if I can't?" he said, moving closer to her.

"Excuse me?" she said, backing away.

"What if I can't, Shemika?" he said insistently. "What if I've fallen for you in a big way? What if you're the girl that I've been looking for?"

"That's ridiculous," she murmured, shaking her head as if to convince herself that what he was saying was nonsense.

"Is it?"

"You're with Kareema," she said breathlessly. "I'm with Touch. We had a moment—"

"Hey," he interrupted, giving her a long, intense look, "it was a lot more than a moment, and you know it."

"No, I don't," she said, totally flustered.

"Yes, you do," he said, moving closer again.

And before either of them realized what was happening, he was touching her shoulder, and somehow his touch turned into an embrace, and the embrace turned into a frenzy of passionate kissing. *I'm sober*, Shemika thought, *and I'm doing this. What's wrong with me?*

But she couldn't stop kissing him, didn't want to. And soon, his hands were on her breasts, and then they were under the silk camisole top she'd changed into as soon as she'd stepped out of the shower. She'd wanted to look pretty for him. Deep down, she'd known this was going to happen.

"*No!*" screamed her inner voice.

"*Yes!*" it screamed back at her.

He started kissing her neck, causing her to shudder with the anticipation of what was to come.

Half-heartedly, she attempted to push him away. "We can't do this," she said in a low voice. "It's not fair to Touch."

"I know," he said, and then he was kissing her again. Somehow or other, they made it to the bedroom, magically losing their clothes along the way.

"You are so fucking perfect," he muttered, rolling on the bed with her, stroking her breasts, kissing her nipples, moving his lips down to her flat stomach, then moving further down and slowly but surely spreading her legs. Within seconds his head was between her thighs, his tongue doing unbelievable things.

She grabbed a pillow, covering her face, waves of desire flooding her senses.

He was taking her on a trip, a trip so exciting and sensual that she could barely contain her groans of sheer pleasure, until finally, she gave it up, moaning with delight as she reached the ultimate peak.

He emerged from between her thighs, hair rumpled, a pleased look on his face. "Good, huh?"

"Beyond good," she murmured, embarrassed to look at him.

"Hey," he said, removing the pillow she was attempting to hide behind, "There's more where that came from."

And then he was moving on top of her, and she made no attempt to stop him. She wanted him inside her. She wanted to feel him close to her.

And once again, it was everything and more, even better than the first time.

After it was over, and they were lying on her bed in the dark, the guilt began creeping back.

"Famous…" she said tentatively.

"What, baby?" he asked, reaching over to touch her.

"This, this isn't right," she said, forcing herself to say the words.

"Feels like it is," he said, stretching lazily.

"No, it isn't. We can't do this."

"Why not?"

"You know why."

"Because of Touch, huh?" he said, wondering if she'd mind if he lit a cigarette, then deciding she definitely would, so he didn't bother asking.

"That's right."

"But Shemika," he said, propping himself up on one elbow and gazing down at her, "you gotta realize that Touch isn't right for you."

"Please listen to me, Famous," she said earnestly. "I can't leave him, not with everything he's going through. Besides, you're with Kareema, and you live in Italy."

"How many times have I gotta tell you?" he said impatiently. "Kareema and I, we're not together."

"You sleep together," she said accusingly.

"Casual sex," he responded.

"What's casual about sex?" she said, frowning. "To me, it's a commitment. A future together. A family. A life."

"Whoa!" he exclaimed. "You are a serious girl."

"I never said I wasn't. And what we're doing is wrong."

"Does it feel wrong?" he asked, stroking her face.

She sat up, reaching for a sheet to cover herself. "Yes," she muttered. "To me, it does."

"You're lying."

"If I am, it's to protect both of us," she said, sighing deeply. "This can't go any further. I mean it."

"Look," he said, "I'm telling Kareema it's over. If it'll make a difference, I'll do it tonight."

"You shouldn't tell her on my account. There is no future for us. I have to stay with Touch."

"Even though you don't love him?" he questioned.

"I never said that."

"You didn't have to."

She started to cry, tears of pure frustration at the situation she found herself in.

Famous reached over and put his arms around her, cradling her against his chest, stroking her hair, and kissing her forehead. "We're gonna work this out," he said quietly. "I promise you, Shemika, we're gonna work this out so that you and I can be together. You know as sure as I do that it's where we both belong."

***

Detective Banks irritated the crap out of Touch. He couldn't stand him with his dumb mustache and intrusive questions. As soon as the two detectives were out of his apartment, Touch poured himself another brandy, his third. Then he knocked on the guest-room door.

Krush was still on the phone talking to his office in L.A. He held up a hand, indicating to Touch that he would be through in a couple of minutes.

Touch stayed in the room, forcing him to curtail his conversation with Chi-rone.

"Here's the latest," Krush said, hanging up. "I have to get back to L.A. tomorrow, so I'm hitching a ride with Chilly Rose."

"You are?" Touch said, trying to hide his disappointment. Having a brother to bond with was a whole new experience and quite a pleasant one.

"It's necessary," Krush explained. "Clients are screaming for my attention, plus I need to deal with my house situation."

"I understand," Touch said.

"You'll be okay?"

"Of course, I will, and I've been thinking."

"Yes?"

"How about I give you the cash I found in Sadiya's box? That way, you can pay off your gambling debt."

"Are you fucking nuts?" Krush exploded, looking at his brother as if he'd totally lost it. "I wouldn't touch that money. Besides, it's not yours, Touch. You have to give it up, hand everything over to the detectives, or at least tell your lawyer about it. Jesus Christ! You're too smart to fuck around like this."

"You think that's what I should do?"

"Damn right. Sadiya was violently murdered. Draygo is obviously a desperate man. Step away."

"I suppose you're right. I should do that."

"When, Touch?"

"Soon."

"I hope so, 'cause this is crazy shit."

"I understand."

"Did you hear from Red yet?"

"Why would I?"

"He must know what happened. It's all over the frigging news. You'd think he'd call."

"Why are you surprised? I'm not."

"Yeah. Typical Red behavior," Krush agreed. "The bastard doesn't give a shit."

"That's right."

"How'd your session with the detective go?"

"He knew I went into the apartment."

"I bet that pissed him off."

72

"Nothing he can do about it now. Oh, and you won't believe this one."

"Go ahead, surprise me."

"Sadiya's personal maid, Irena, the old Russian woman that I can't stand? It turns out she's probably Sadiya's mother."

"No way," Krush said.

"Apparently so. I think I should talk to her."

"Why would you want to do that?"

"She might know something she's not telling the police, something about Draygo."

"Shit!" Krush snapped. "Aren't you listening to me? You've gotta stop this crap. They're going to find out about Draygo whatever you do."

"You think so?"

"Look," Krush said patiently, "give the detectives the box with everything in it, including the money. And remember, they're the detectives, not you. Do it soon, Touch, because I do not want to be the one bailing you out of jail for holding back evidence."

"That won't happen."

"I hope you're right. I really hope you're right."

***

The Russian gangster was strong, brawny, and rough, with big meaty hands to match his big meaty dick.

Isha would never admit it to anyone but herself, but she was quite into being dominated. It made a welcome change from all the old men she slept with for money. Old rich men with tired dicks and kinky tastes. A good old-fashioned fuck with a manly man made quite a welcome change. Until Alex Pinchinoff stuffed his enormous member into her mouth and attempted to choke her.

That was the moment she remembered why she hadn't wanted to see him again.

At least this time, he hadn't insisted on handcuffing her, and he was attractive in a sinister kind of way. Tall, with heavy-set features, thick black hair, and dominating eyebrows. For a moment, she fantasized what it would be like to be married to a man like Alex. He'd want to fuck her every day, knock her up with a kid or two, expect her to cook and clean, and give him regular blowjobs. Then he'd take a mistress, a young American blonde with a tight little pussy and a big American smile.

Fantasy over.

She managed to give him head without gagging. Then he fucked her again until they both came for the second time, and she lay there quite spent.

"You pleased to see me tonight?" he asked, lighting up a foul-smelling dark brown cigarette.

They were in the bedroom of his mostly red apartment: red-painted walls, red carpet, even red sheets.

"You're not bad," she allowed with a faint smile.

His big hand went straight to her landing strip of dyed pubic hair, which he proceeded to tug. "I'll make you come?"

"Yes."

"Not too big for you?"

"No."

"You interesting woman. Who are those morons you with tonight?"

"They're not morons," she said, defending Igor and Draygo. "One of them is my cousin. The other guy was the husband of a murdered rich woman. He'll get all her money."

"What woman?" Alex asked, his interest piqued.

"Murdered Russian woman in newspapers," Isha replied, wondering where in the hell Alex had come across red sheets.

"Paulina Kuchinova?" he questioned, blowing a stream of foul smoke in her direction.

"You know her real name?" Isha said, surprised. Maybe Draygo was telling the truth after all. Who would've thought it? "How do you know her real name?"

"I know more than her name?" Alex said, vigorously scratching his balls. "That bitch owes me plenty of money. Whoever killed her did a fine job. That was one greedy bitch who had it coming. Ah, yes," he added, nodding to himself. "I knew Paulina. I knew her well. So, you tell me where I can find Draygo cause now he owes me plenty of money."

Von Diesel

Chapter Eight

Velvet had a dilemma. Should she go to dinner with Savage and the gang or spend the evening with Tristin and Parker J. Jones, her soon-to-be producer? She didn't want to offend Savage; he'd been so great towards her. On the other hand, Tristin was in L.A. and, married or not, how could she resist spending time with him?

Away from New York, things seemed cooler. It was almost like she was on vacation where nothing mattered except having a good time. Not that she'd ever been on vacation, it was a luxury she'd missed out on.

Wow! So much going on, and all of it is unbelievable. If it wasn't for her mother ruining everything, she'd be flying high.

Tristin was staying in the same hotel. What a surprise! She'd told him she'd call him in five minutes.

First, she buzzed Holliday's room to check if it was okay to bring Tristin and Parker to dinner.

"Tristin Juzang, the hip-hop king?" Holliday asked, sounding impressed. "First Tony A, now Tristin Juzang. Didn't you tell me you were a new girl on the scene?"

"I am."

"Someone's been making up stories."

"Tony A is a friend from way back," Velvet explained. "And Tristin's putting me together with Parker J. Jones, the record producer."

"I'm sure Savage won't mind," Holliday said. "Want me to call him for you?"

"Would you? Then get straight back to me."

Within seconds, Holliday was on the phone again. "Savage is down with it." Now she had to ask Tristin if he'd mind joining her friends for dinner. She called him. "A group scene?" Tristin quipped. "Naw, not for me. I'm into up-close and personal, just the two of us."

"Be serious," she scolded. "Savage is the photographer I'm working with, and the others are fun. I'd love it if you and Parker could join us. Later, we can talk about my music."

"Talk about her music, the girl says," Tristin drawled. "Sure, babe. That's exactly what I flew to L.A. for, to talk about your music."

"You brought a producer with you, didn't you?"

"Yeah."

"So?"

"So, we'll come to dinner."

"Seven-thirty in the lobby."

"How many limos should I order?"

"How many what?"

"Limos, to get to the restaurant."

"I'm sure we can grab a cab."

"Nobody takes cabs in L.A."

"Maybe you should meet us at the restaurant. It's Ivy at the Shore."

"Hey, LL, you do know I got on a plane specially to see you, so don't go giving me no 'I'll catch up with you later' shit."

"I didn't ask you to come here."

"It'll be worth it."

"You think?"

He laughed. "Yeah."

"Really?" she said. "But you still have a ring on your finger, right?"

"Man," he complained. "You sure are playing hard to get."

"I'm being honest with you. Seems people being honest with you doesn't happen very often."

"You noticed," he said wryly.

"You're incredibly hot, Tristin," she said, deciding to throw him off guard because, in spite of what Chanel thought, she knew a thing or two about dealing with men. "And if you were single," she continued, "there's no way we'd be having this conversation."

"We wouldn't, huh?" he said, intrigued.

"No," she said boldly. "We'd be rolling around on a bed having insanely wild sex."

"Now she's trying to excite me over the phone," he groaned. "And it's working. You into phone sex, babe?"

"No, thanks," she said crisply. "And, believe me, I am not trying to excite you. I'm simply telling you the way it is because if you flew here to sleep with me, you could forget it."

"Man, you're a tough one," he grumbled.

"It's called self-preservation."

"So that's what it's called."

"Reverse the roles, and you'll get it."

"Smart too."

"I try."

"Well, LL, you think you can ride with me to the restaurant?"

"I'm supposed to meet everybody in the lobby at seven-thirty."

"I'll come to get you at seven-fifteen. We'll arrive early, grab a mojito or two."

She called Holliday back and told him they were coming and that they'd all meet up at the restaurant.

"Miss. Thang!" Holliday exclaimed delightedly. "You know absolutely everybody. I am sooo impressed!"

***

After an awkward start, everyone got along well. Velvet had to admit that Tristin possessed charm and then some. He was warm and friendly, and in no way at all did he play the 'I'm a big hip-hop record mogul' role.

Parker J. Jones, a big man with a matching personality, was a riot. It turned out he'd produced records for Brandy, Chilly Rose, Toni Braxton, and a host of other female stars.

Holliday and Quinn were all over him, and even Uma was fascinated by his stories, especially the Chilly Rose ones. Uma was obsessed with Chilly Rose. She listened avidly as Parker confided that Chilly was a major pop tart diva, with outrageous demands, including serious perks for whatever hunk she was banging at the time.

Savage and Tristin bonded. They were both into cars. Savage had recently purchased his first Ferrari, a 575 Maranello, and it turned out Tristin owned three very special Ferraris, including the new Superamerica and a Maserati.

"Man, I gotta photograph you with your cars," Savage said enthusiastically. "For sure, it's a *Rolling Stone* cover. Or *Vanity Fair*. Graydon will definitely get off on the car thing."

"Don't wanna disappoint, but I'm not into doing much personal PR," Tristin admitted. "I kinda leave that shit to my wife."

He caught Velvet listening and was sorry he'd mentioned the word wife.

Screw him, Velvet thought, freezing up. After two glasses of wine, she'd started thinking about what could happen between them. Then, when she heard the wife's comment, it was over. Determinedly she turned her attention to Parker, where it should've been in the first place. After all, Parker was her future. He was the one who was going to help make sure she sounded great.

"Did you get a chance to listen to my demo?" she asked him.

"That's why I'm here," Parker said, enjoying a dish of crab cakes.

"Listened to it with Tristin, and I liked what I heard. I wouldn't have flown to L.A. if I hadn't. Although I gotta say, any time I can hitch a ride on Tristin's plane, it's kinda hard t" say no. You bin on it?"

"I haven't."

"Well, then, little lady, you got yourself one big fucking treat waiting for you. That dude sure knows how to treat himself like a king."

"So, you really liked my demo?" she asked, steering the conversation back to her music.

"With a few reservations," Parker said. "Nothing we can't fix."

"Reservations?" she asked, alarmed. "Like what?"

"You gotta think about your material. Right now, it's too damn dark and gloomy. And remember, you ain't no Alicia Keys, so stop trying to copy her style. She's an original, and that's what you're gonna be."

"I'm not copying anyone," she objected.

"Now don't go getting defensive on me," Parker warned, "because we gotta lot work to do together. Big lesson, learn to listen to criticism and take it in 'cause if you can't do that, we ain't going nowhere. Are we understanding each other?"

She nodded, suitably chastised. Parker was a professional. She wasn't.

Not yet. She would do as he said, listen and learn.

Hopefully, it will all work out.

Driving back to the hotel, Velvet found herself alone in the limo with Tristin.

"Where's Parker?" she asked, a touch breathlessly. "I thought he was coming with us."

Tristin laughed. "Yeah, well, here's the deal. Parker's got himself a hot little honey he keeps stashed in Beverly Hills. That's the real reason he flew to L.A. on such short notice."

"I thought I was the reason," she joked.

"Yeah, yeah, no offense, but he ain't gonna get no sweet juice outta you."

"Is he married?"

"There she goes again." Tristin sighed, shaking his head. "What are you? A secret rep for the moral majority?"

"Can't help it if I have principles," she said, smiling lightly.

"Guess that means I'm not getting any tonight."

"Tonight. Tomorrow night. You know why."

"Yeah, yeah. I know," he said ruefully. "I'm married. And it doesn't mean anything to you that my wife and I, we got ourselves an arrangement."

"Not what I heard."

"Yeah? What did you hear?"

"That your wife would beat any girl's head in with her eight-hundred-dollar Manolos if she caught you playing. Apparently, she's fierce."

Tristin burst out laughing. "My wife wouldn't do anything with them Manolos if she thought it might damage them. She's a shoe-whore, baby. A shoe-whore all the way."

"Whatever," Velvet said, leaning back against the leather seat, thinking, who would've believed less than a week ago that I'd be sitting in a limo in L.A. with Tristin Juzang himself. It's too much!

"I've been meaning to ask you something. How come you don't sound like no other black chicks I know?" Tristin asked, reaching o and taking her hand.

"I don't?"

"You know you don't."

"I guess it's because my mom got a job uptown, pulled me out of school in Harlem, and sent me to a fancy one in Manhattan," she explained, carefully withdrawing her hand from his. "I hated the new school, and everyone hated me. I didn't fit in, but I suppose that's where I learned to speak properly."

"What does your mom do?"

"She was a singer," Velvet said and hesitated. Then she continued, "Uh...now she's a housekeeper to some crappy old billionaire."

"A billionaire, huh? The kinda dude I might know?"

"Red Bentley. His son's ex-wife was found stabbed to death this week."

"Jeez! That story is everywhere. There's a panic run on hiring security guards."

"There is?"

"What's the real scam?"

Velvet shrugged. "Beats me."

"You mean your mom didn't go inside?"

"I haven't asked her."

"No, you wouldn't."

"What do you mean by that?"

"Too many principles to go digging for dirt, right?"

"Something wrong with that?"

"Don't sweat it. You're an original, babe, and I'm into originals."

The limo pulled into the driveway of the hotel, and Tristin helped her out. "Here's the plan," he said. "We're gonna take a romantic stroll along the beach."

"First of all, you and I are not romantic. It's late. I have to be up early, and—"

"How many excuses are you gonna come up with?" he asked, looking amused. "Relax, LL, it's not often you get to do this kinda thing."

"Well…" she said unsurely.

"C'mon, babe," he said, guiding her through a side gate. "Live dangerously, or you're not living at all."

As they hit the vast expanse of sand that led down to the ocean, he bent down and started taking his Nikes off.

She slipped out of the silver sandals Uma had given her that morning and rolled up her cargo pants. When she was done, Tristin grabbed her hand and began running with her down the beach towards the ocean. The sand felt smooth and cool beneath her bare feet, and the sound of the waves crashing on the shore was quite hypnotizing. She felt invigorated and alive, realizing that this was a night to savor.

When they were almost at the ocean, he stopped, pulled her to him, and, without saying a word, began to kiss her.

She found herself powerless to say no. What did it really matter that he was married? She wasn't planning a long love affair with him. Anyway, he'd told her that he and his wife had an arrangement, so why not?

No! She knew enough about men and their desires to realize that he was only offering to help her with her career because she was playing hard to get. A man like Tristin could probably sleep with any woman he chose. He had it all, looks, power, money, not to mention a fleet of Ferraris, and, to top it all off, his own plane.

Tristin Juzang had everything most women wanted. But he didn't have her. And that's what made her different.

She was thinking all this while they kissed, his tongue exciting her senses, but not enough that she was about to succumb to his advances.

"You're a great kisser," she said breathlessly, breaking apart from him. "But my call tomorrow is six a.m., so I'm heading back to the hotel."

"You are?" he said, surprised. She was right; turn downs were not an everyday occurrence in Tristin's life.

She started walking, then turned and called out, "Coming?"

"Yeah, in my pants," he muttered, chasing after her, once more grabbing her hand. "You are something else, LL."

"I'll take that as a compliment."

"You do that."

They made it to the lobby, windswept and out of breath. And there stood Tony A, in all his white-suited and streaked-spiky-hair glory, an uptight Hector hovering by his side.

"Where have you been?" Tony asked, stepping forward with a proprietary air about him. "I thought we'd arranged to get together?"

"She's been with me," Tristin said, jumping aggressively into the picture. "So...you got something to say, then say it to me, dude."

Von Diesel

Chapter Nine

First thing Wednesday morning, Mrs. Conner appeared in the kitchen. Touch had already been up for a couple of hours, unable to sleep. Try as he might, he couldn't forget the vivid image of Sadiya sprawled on her bed in a pool of blood.

For a while, he'd attempted to work on his computer, but there was too much on his mind for him to concentrate on business. So many questions, and how was he supposed to find the answers?

In a way, it would be a relief if Draygo turned up at his office, but he had a feeling the man would lie low for a while, stay out of sight.

He'd made up his mind that today he would contact Irena, go see her and listen to what she had to say. If she was Sadiya's mother, then she might be the one with the answers to all his questions.

Finally, he'd abandoned doing any work and gone into the kitchen to make coffee, which was where Mrs. Conner found him.

"Good morning, Mr. Bentley," Mrs. Conner said, bustling in and taking over the coffee-making duty.

"You're up early," he remarked, glancing at his watch, noting it was a few minutes before seven.

"I've always been an early riser," Mrs. Conner said, filling the coffeemaker with water. "In my hometown of Glasgow, seven o'clock was considered far too late for a person to be getting their lazy selves out of bed." "Where's Camryn?" he asked, suppressing a yawn.

"The girl is still asleep," Mrs. Conner responded. "The two of us had quite an afternoon yesterday. I took her to the park, then we stopped for ice cream, and after that, she came to the market with me and picked out all her favorite cereals and cookies."

"She enjoys spending time with you," Touch commented.

"And me with her," Mrs. Conner answered. "She's a beautiful little girl. This tragedy is such a shame—"

"Let's not discuss it, Mrs. Conner," he said, cutting her off. "I think it's a subject we should consider closed as far as Camryn is concerned."

"I hate to say this, Mr. Bentley, but she's bound to find out as soon as she goes back to school. When we arrived home yesterday, there were reporters and camera crews outside the building. I shielded the wee babe as best I could, but they were yelling things at her."

"Jesus Christ!" he said furiously. "Can't they leave anyone alone?"

"I have a suggestion, Mr. Bentley. My sister works for a family in Montauk. They live in a lovely house right on the beach, and they've gone off to Europe for a month. They told my sister that I could stay with her. I thought, if you approve, I might take Camryn there for a few days. It will be quiet, and it would certainly get the little one away from all this fuss and bother."

"That sounds good, Mrs. Conner. How does Camryn feel about it?"

"I waited to ask you first, but I think she'd have quite a time. My sister has twins, two wee ones only a few months younger than Camryn."

"If she wants to go, then take her," Touch said, quite relieved. "I haven't even started interviewing nannies yet. I was hoping you'd stay with her until things settle down."

"It'll be my pleasure, Mr. Bentley. Excuse me now. I must go see if our little princess is stirring." She bustled off.

A few minutes later, Krush came into the kitchen. "I'm packed and ready to go," he announced.

"Back to your non-existent house?" Touch asked.

"It's not as bad as I thought," Krush said, pouring himself a mug of coffee. "Chi-rone tells me the rain has finally stopped, and they're dredging the mud from my house. So, as soon as everything's been cleaned, if it's not dangerous, I can move back in."

"Listen," Touch said, "that was no idle promise when I said I'd loan you the money to get you out of trouble with that guy in Vegas."

"Really?" Krush said, taking a couple of gulps of hot coffee. "You'd do that?"

"Wouldn't say it if I didn't mean it. How much do you need?"

"Well, Chi-rone recovered my safe," Krush said, "and there's two hundred and fifty thousand in there, so another three hundred and fifty will do it."

"Consider it taken care of."

"Thanks, Touch. I'm planning to be in Vegas this weekend for Chilly's wedding. Man, you don't know what a freaking pleasure it'll be to get Roth off my case."

"I can imagine," Touch said.

"So," Krush said, pouring himself more coffee, "the Japanese are on board, your project is going ahead, everything's cool."

"It's all good," Touch agreed. "Back to business as usual."

"Don't forget what we talked about last night. Hand the box over, tell them Sadiya left it with you for safe-keeping, and you forgot about it. If they think you took it out of her apartment, you'll be in deep shit. Trust me on this."

Touch nodded. He was aware that Krush was right, but at the same time, he had to talk to Irena before he did anything.

Camryn bounded into the kitchen. "Can I go to the beach with Mrs. Conner, Daddy? Can I? Can I? Can I?" she asked excitedly, hopping up and down.

"Yes, sweetie, if that's what you'd like."

"Yes, Daddy, that's what Camryn wants. No school! No! No! No! Mrs. Conner is my favorite."

"When am I gonna be your favorite?" Krush asked, bending down to give her a hug.

"Let me see," Camryn said, with a cheeky smile, "you can be my favorite tomorrow."

"Can't wait!" Krush replied, winking at Touch. "I always dreamed of meeting a girl like you."

Camryn dissolved into a fit of childish giggles.

***

Shemika stirred in her sleep and threw out her arm. She was startled to hit another body. Then it all came rushing back. She was in bed with Famous.

Somehow or other, he'd ended up spending the night.

Oh, God! What had she done now? Wasn't the first time bad enough?

He was still asleep, snoring lightly. She stared down at his face. He was so handsome, and it wasn't just his looks that got her. It was the way he was with her. Last night they'd talked for hours. Other than Megan, he was the first person she'd confided in about her kidnapping ordeal, and it had been such a relief sharing the experience that she'd ended up telling him everything.

"Didn't you ever see a shrink about it?" he'd asked.

"No, my mother told me I had to forget it ever happened."

"The woman is freaking crazy," Famous had said. "She should've immediately gotten you some help."

"Unfortunately, she didn't."

"That's why you've always been repressed sexually."

"You think I'm sexually repressed?"

"Until we got together, you were a twenty-one-year-old virgin living in New York. You consider that normal?"

"I, I don't know."

"Believe me; it's not. You were sexually molested at fourteen, Shemika, and that made you terrified of sex."

"Then why aren't I terrified of you?"

"Because we have this amazing chemistry thing going."

"We do?" she'd said shyly.

"That, or you were totally wasted," he'd teased. "It's certainly the reason you've held Touch off."

"You think so?"

"It's a sure thing. It fits right into his hang-up."

"What's his hang-up?"

"He didn't tell you?"

"Tell me what?"

"I only know the story from Krush, but apparently, when Touch was in high school, he had a steady girlfriend. The night of the junior prom, he brought her back to the house. Red walked in on them just as they were about to do it."

"Oh, no!"

"Red started yelling and screaming, sent Touch to his room, then the old pervert proceeded to rape the girl. She was sixteen."

"What?" Shemika had gasped. "That's so awful."

"And that is why he's so not into sex. So, you see, the two of you made the perfect pair."

"He never told me about it."

"Hey, if you and Touch had any kind of connection, you'd both know everything about each other, wouldn't you?"

"I feel so bad for him now."

"Cut it out. Touch isn't right for you, and you've got to break it off."

"I can't tell him about us, Famous. I can't."

"You'll do it, eventually. Or he'll find out by himself. We'll sneak around for a while, that's all."

"I don't want to sneak around."

"Not forever," Famous had assured her. "One day, we'll bring it out into the open. By that time, Touch will have found someone else, so it won't break his heart."

"You don't understand," she'd said plaintively. "Touch loves me. He really loves me."

"He loves you because you're Miss Pure. Don't you get it? Nobody can touch you except him. That's what he loves about you, Shemika."

Eventually, they'd fallen asleep on top of the tangled sheets, and now it was morning.

"Famous," Shemika murmured softly, catching a glimpse of the bedside clock, "it's almost eight. We slept right through."

He struggled to open his eyes. "Oh, shit," he mumbled.

"What?"

"Kareema's gonna be pissed. I should've let her know I wasn't coming home last night."

"I thought you told me you had an open relationship."

"We do, but ever since she's been in New York, she's been kind of clingy. It's...difficult."

"I have to get to work," Shemika said, climbing out of bed. "And you should go do what you have to do."

"I'll come over later."

"No."

"Why not?"

"Because this is all happening too fast," she said, feeling confused. "I don't want to sneak around like you said. As it is, Krush knows, and how do you think that makes me feel?"

"Krush doesn't know."

"Don't lie to me, Famous."

"Uh...well, maybe I mentioned that I like you."

"I'm not an idiot. You told him, didn't you?" she said accusingly.

"It was a mistake," he admitted. "I was so shocked when I saw you at the rehearsal dinner. I've been talking about you non-stop. Krush knew I was looking for a girl, and then she turned out to be you."

"You were talking about me?" she asked softly. "Looking for me?"

"From the moment you ran out of my apartment," he said, pulling her back to bed.

"Yes?"

"You bet."

"Oh, Famous." She sighed. "What are we going to do?"

"We're going to be very, very happy, and that, my sweet girl, is a promise."

***

Touch made the trek to Brighton Beach, where Irena lived in a run-down apartment building surrounded by shops, Russian restaurants, and seedy-looking nightclubs.

Since he hadn't wanted his driver to know where he was going, he'd driven himself in his usual erratic style.

He'd discovered Irena's address in Sadiya's phone book and, next to it, a phone number. He'd tried the number several times, but nobody had answered, so he'd taken a chance and driven out to see her.

Now he stood outside the crumbling old apartment building, wishing he would have persuaded Krush to come with him. There was something surreal about being in this place. It was as though he'd stepped out of Manhattan into a completely different world, a world of grey skies, stormy ocean breezes drifting in from the nearby beach, drizzling rain, and run-down storefronts.

Krush was right. Why hadn't he handed everything over to Detective Banks and backed away? He was a businessman, not a goddamn detective.

A line of grimy mailboxes informed him that Irena's apartment was on the fifth floor. The elevator bore a 'NOT WORKING' cardboard sign, so he took the concrete stairs. A strong stink of cat piss, stale beer, and old cooking smells pervaded the air. If Irena was Sadiya's mother, then Sadiya sure as hell hadn't cared much about her living conditions.

When he reached the apartment, he could hear music playing, loud, strident sounds that were unfamiliar to his ears. There was no doorbell, so he knocked. Once. Twice. Louder.

Nobody came.

An old man in grey pajamas, with a matching beard and a workman's cap perched jauntily on his head, opened the door of the apartment across the hall, and muttered something in Russian, at least Touch presumed it was Russian.

"Excuse me?" Touch said.

"Not so much noise," the old man grumbled in thickly accented English.

"Is the woman who lives in this apartment home?" Touch asked, speaking slowly in a louder-than-usual voice.

"No English," the old man shouted, retreating back into his place as Irena opened the door to hers.

She stood for a moment, her face frozen with shock. She was a stout, homely-looking woman with frizzed greyish hair and a florid complexion. "Mr. Bentley," she said, at last, her mouth popping open in surprise. "What do you do here?"

"Came to see you, Irena. Can I come in?"

Reluctantly she allowed him into her one cramped room with an unmade bed in the corner, a hot plate, and an old-fashioned icebox. An ancient black and white TV blared loudly while a mangy cat lay sleeping contentedly on its back.

Irena switched off the TV and flapped her hands in the air. "Mrs. Bentley," she lamented. "Such a terrible thing. So terrible..."

As he stood awkwardly in the middle of the room, he noticed a sudden sparkle on Irena's pinky finger. It emanated from a very large Bentley ring. The ring he had presented Sadiya with on the day they got engaged.

***

When Famous burst into Eddie's apartment, Kareema was busy packing. "Hey!" he said.

She barely glanced in his direction.

"Uh, sorry about last night," he began. "It was—"

"Nothing," she interrupted, bestowing an ice-cold look on him.

"Nothing?" he said, taking a crumpled pack of cigarettes from his pocket.

"We finished, Famous, you and I. Finished. Over. Arrivederci."

Yeah, they were the words he wanted to hear, but he was the one supposed to be saying them, not Kareema.

"I gotta explain what happened," he said, lighting up a much-needed cigarette.

"No, Famous," Kareema said, folding an expensive embroidered skirt and placing it in one of her suitcases. "You made me look stupida in front of Alexia. Kareema no like that."

"I'm sorry," he said, inhaling deeply.

"Too late, baby," she said, tossing back her long auburn hair.

"Incredibile!"

"I was with Touch," he lied.

"No," she said, eyes flashing dangerously. "I call Touch, you no there. You possibly are with some girl, and that's non importa. But how do you say stand me up? Oh no, no, no! You cannot do that to Kareema."

"So, you're leaving?"

"Sì," she said abruptly, slamming shut the last of her suitcases.

He didn't know what to say. Kareema was leaving, and that was exactly what he wanted. So why did he feel at a loss, empty, as if she was abandoning him?

Could it be because the only home he had was hers? The only place he'd been really settled and happy was Milan? The only career he had going was in Italy.

Right now, he was living in Eddie's apartment, he had no steady job, and Shemika was shying away from making a commitment.

Apparently, he didn't have much of anything. And Kareema was leaving.

The beautiful, capricious, fun-loving, incredibly sexy Kareema.

What would he do without her? How would he survive?

Don't panic, he thought. I'll be fine. I'll get hooked up with an agent in New York, rent an apartment, and eventually, I'll be with Shemika.

The downstairs buzzer rang.

"My car," Kareema said, still icing him out. "Kindly tell the driver to come up for my luggage."

"Are you sure you want to do this?" he asked, shocked that she was walking out on him.

"Si, Famous," she answered, not even looking at him. "Kareema is leaving. And Kareema will not be coming back."

***

Krush had almost made it to the airport when he got the call on his cell. Red Bentley was on the phone. His caring, loving father.

"Where are you?" Red demanded as if they were in constant contact, and he was entitled to know.

"I'm on my way back to L.A.," Krush answered, surprised that his father had found him, although Red Bentley had always possessed a nose for tracking his prey.

"You flew to New York to meet with me," Red pointed out, sounding calm for such a crotchety old bastard. "Now you're leaving without doing so. Is that smart?"

"I'm leaving because I have a business to take care of," Krush said. "And our meeting never worked out, did it?"

"You ran out on me."

"I left you to be with Touch. I'm sure you heard that his ex-wife was murdered in her apartment, or did you miss that piece of news?"

"We have to reschedule," Red said, ignoring the reference to Sadiya's demise.

"I don't know when I'll be back in New York," Krush said. "So, you can forget it."

"Doesn't suit me," Red replied. "Tomorrow. Ten a.m. My house."

"Didn't I just tell you that I'm on my way to L.A.?" Krush said, exasperated. "I'm five minutes away from the airport. There's a plane waiting for me."

"Too bad," Red said abruptly.

"Too bad what?" Krush said, getting hooked in.

"Too bad you can't be there to listen to what I have to tell the three of you."

"What do you have to tell us, Dad, that we don't already know?" Krush said, getting ready to spill some of the venom he'd been holding in for so many years. "You want to tell us how useless we are? What a bunch of fuckups we turned out to be? How did you always know that we'd never amount to anything? Is that what your meeting is all about?"

"If you're any kind of a businessman, you'll be there," Red said. "Especially if you're interested in hearing the true story behind your mother's unfortunate death."

And, without further ado, Red Bentley hung up.

Chapter Ten

Isha did not leave Alex's garish red apartment until noon on Wednesday.

The night before, he'd asked her to stay over, so she'd done so, interested in listening to his diatribe about Sadiya Bentley, born Paulina Kochinova. According to Alex, he'd met Paulina at a club when she'd first arrived in New York. He'd fallen in lust, followed by love. Paulina/Sadiya had claimed she felt the same about him, but he was soon to learn that a Russian Mob guy was not good enough for Sadiya. No. She wanted more, and before long, she had her hooks into Touch Bentley, a real-estate tycoon with excellent social standing. While dating Touch, she'd managed to string Alex along, seeing both men, sleeping with both men. Then one day, to Alex's fury, marrying Touch. After that, she would only meet with him sporadically until the divorce, and then she'd come back into Alex's life, claiming she'd always loved him, and they belonged together. But only if they kept their affair a secret until she received the full pay-out on her divorce settlement. They started seeing each other again on a semi-regular basis, but not in public unless it was at one of the Russian clubs Alex frequented. Then Sadiya would arrive wearing a black wig and revert to her real name, Paulina.

The sex between them was frantic: hot and dirty, the way they both liked it. After a while, Sadiya suggested she might be able to help him business-wise. She knew he dealt in stolen gemstones, and who better to broker them for him than a woman high up on the social scale?

So, they went into business together, and for a while, it worked perfectly until Sadiya decided to screw him out of several important and valuable stones and a shitload of cash.

"She found another rich man to take care of her. She didn't need me anymore," Alex told Isha, his mouth set in a grim line. "She told me she loved me, promised we would be together. Then she stole from me, the bitch stole from me, Alex Pinchinoff. She deserved to die."

Lying next to him in bed, Isha had shivered and wondered if it was Alex who murdered Sadiya.

She'd then decided it couldn't be him because Alex wouldn't have stabbed her; he would have suffocated her with his giant cock.

After taking in his story, Isha had sensed there was money to be made, major money. Sadiya Bentley had been murdered, a big society woman with many important connections, not the least being that she'd once been married to real-estate tycoon Touch Bentley, whose father happened to be Red Bentley, the old billionaire whom she and Inka had spent the previous weekend fucking.

And yet, according to Igor, Draygo, and Alex Pinchinoff, Sadiya Bentley had originally been Paulina Kuchinova, a one-time Moscow prostitute who'd been married to Draygo, and they'd never been divorced! Now there was Alex's story to add to the mix, although Isha realized it would be fatal to name Alex.

Isha was smart enough to realize that the money-making possibilities were endless. Sadiya Bentley's murder was already headline news. What if people found out the real truth?

The story was explosive, and she, little Isha Parker, was sitting on it. But not for long: if she didn't act fast, Draygo, Igor, or Alex might blow it.

Once she got home, she considered her alternatives. Sell the story to a tabloid newspaper. Or...see if Touch Bentley was prepared to pay even more to keep the scandal from rocking his uptight world. She remembered Touch from his bachelor party; he was no pushover like his brother, Krush, or the insatiable, Viagra-popping, foul-mouthed Red.

How much would Touch Bentley be prepared to pay to keep the story out of the press? Enough for her to retire? Take the money and move somewhere far away, where the others, Draygo, Igor, and Alex, couldn't find her? Because eventually, they'd catch on that there was money to be made. And by that time, it would be too late. She would've already scored.

Hmmm... It was all about timing and speed. She had to move quickly before it was too late, and Draygo springs forward as Sadiya's legal husband so that he could claim her estate. Before Alex realized he was sitting on a hot story about his illicit love affair with the big society woman and before Igor screwed everything up, as usual.

By Wednesday afternoon, she'd made her decision. She would go to Red Bentley before anyone else. She'd tell him what she knew and the price for her silence. Red would definitely want to protect his family's name and his little granddaughter, whom she'd seen pictured all over the newspapers. The advantage was that she knew how to contact Red directly; she'd jotted down his cell number when she and Inka had spent the weekend in his apartment.

And if he didn't want to pay, too bad, she'd go straight to one of the tabloid newspapers.

No problem. They would be happy to pay for a story as juicy as this.

***

"Hi," Krush said into his cell. "Sorry, Chilly, I can't make it. You'd better take off without me." He'd already instructed his driver to turn the car around and head back to the city.

"Bummer!" Chilly squealed. "I get off being with you, Krush. You're like my totally fave older man."

Older man? He was thirty-two, for Christ's sake. Since when was thirty-two considered 'older'?

"It's business, Chilly," he explained. "I'll see you in Vegas. Oh, yes, and there'll be papers coming over to you for Brewsky to sign. Make sure he does, or there'll be no wedding."

"You're missing out, Krush," Chilly cooed. "I've got two hotties on the plane with me, and one of them totally gets off on—"

"What?" he interrupted. "Old farts?"

"No, silly." She giggled. "Lawyers."

Yeah, that was all he needed to do, hook up with one of Chilly's manic teenage sex-crazed girlfriends.

"Guess she'll have to wait until Vegas," he said, thinking about his manipulative father and what he'd like to do to him.

"I'll tell her," Chilly promised. "But she's gonna be very disappointed."

"I'm sure she'll live."

Much as he'd felt the urge to get back to L.A., there was another, stronger urge pulling him towards Manhattan and a father he couldn't stand. A father who'd said, especially if you're interested in hearing the true story behind your mother's unfortunate death.

Yes. He was desperate to hear the true story. There'd always been a lack of information about his mother's plane crash, just as there was a lack of information about the demise of Touch's mother from a so-called heart attack in her twenties.

Could it be that Red had somehow orchestrated the two women's deaths?

No. Not even Red Bentley would be capable of such evil. Or would he?

***

"You wanted to see me?" Fatima said, standing uncomfortably in the doorway of Lady J Bentley's room.

"Yes, I do," Lady Bentley said, waving an arm imperiously in the air. "Come in. Close the door behind you."

Fatima did as the woman requested. She had heard the arguments between Lady Bentley and Red Bentley. She had witnessed him screaming venom at the woman, telling her to get out. Everyone on the staff had hoped that this was it, the end of Lady Bentley and her unreasonable demands. But no. Days later, she was still in residence, firmly ensconced in her tastefully decorated bedroom. She had not even begun to pack.

"How can I help you, Lady Bentley?" Fatima asked, determined to remain calm in the face of anything this bigoted, loathsome woman had to say.

Lady Bentley gave her a long, appraising look. "How old are you?" she asked.

"Excuse me?"

"How old are you?" Lady Bentley repeated. "It's not such a difficult question, is it?"

Fatima thought about telling the woman it was none of her damn business and fleeing the room. After all, what could Lady Bentley do to her? She certainly couldn't fire her: Fatima was under Red Bentley's employ, and he would never let her go.

But something made her stay and answer the question, and she wasn't sure why.

"Thirty-eight," she said, at last, dying to add, "Younger than you," but she controlled the impulse.

"Thirty-eight," Lady Bentley repeated. "And how long have you worked here?"

"Almost ten years."

"So, you were quite a young woman when you decided to give up your singing career, such as it was, and come to work for Mr. Bentley or Red, as I'm sure you called him in the early days when you were sleeping with him."

Fatima felt a moment of sheer panic. No one knew about her dealings with Red Bentley, dealings that had started long before she became his housekeeper. It was a private matter between them, and they both had their reasons to make sure it stayed that way.

"I beg your pardon?" Fatima said, keeping her voice neutral.

"I bet you do, beg my pardon," Lady Bentley sneered, a vindictive gleam in her eyes. "All these years, I imagined Red was out whoring around, but now I discover he had his own black whore, right here, stashed downstairs for his convenience whenever he wished to avail himself of her services."

"I have no idea what you're talking about," Fatima said, knowing she had to get out of this woman's room as fast as possible.

"Please, spare me the innocent act," Lady Bentley said. "I know everything. Everything." A long, silent beat. "Do you understand me?"

"I understand that we shouldn't be having this conversation," Fatima muttered. "Mr. Bentley wouldn't like it."

"Oh, wouldn't he?" Lady Bentley said bitterly. "Too damn bad." Fatima turned to leave the room.

"I know your secret," Lady Bentley taunted. "I know your dirty little secret. So, if you're wise, I suggest you encourage Red to give me everything my lawyer has requested, and maybe–just maybe–your secret will stay safe with me."

Unnerved by her meeting with Lady Bentley, Fatima hurried downstairs to her apartment and tried calling Velvet in L.A. There was no answer from her daughter's hotel room.

This was all so unsettling and unexpected. Nobody knew about her connection to Red Bentley. Nobody. And certainly not Velvet.

How had Lady Bentley found out? And what proof did she have, if any?

Lady Bentley was claiming she knew things that nobody except she and Red was privy to.

This wasn't possible. And yet…

***

"Where have you been?"

"Huh?" Famous mumbled, cradling the phone. He was sitting in Eddie's apartment trying to come to grips with the fact that Kareema had walked out on him. This was a first, and even though it saved him the trouble, he was not sure he liked it.

"Who's this?" he managed.

"Krush. Who did you think it was?"

"Uh…"

"What's up with you? Have you been drinking?"

"No way."

"You sound fucked up."

"I'm not."

"Then where have you been?" Krush repeated. "I've left messages. Don't you return calls?"

"My phone's on vibrate."

"Great. Well, check your messages. There's probably one from Red."

"How come?"

"Cause he's summoning us to another meeting. Wants us all there at ten tomorrow, his house."

"Are we going?"

"You bet your ass we're going. I just blew out a flight back to L.A., so I can be there."

"What makes you think he will?" Famous asked. "He's the fucking king of the jack-offs. You saw him the other day walking in with those two hookers."

"He'll be there," Krush said. "He's got something on his mind that he needs us to hear."

"Who gives a shit?" Famous muttered.

"Have you called Touch?"

"Touch," Famous said blankly. "Why would I call him?"

"Jesus!" Krush exclaimed, suddenly realizing what was going on. "You're seeing Shemika, aren't you?"

"What makes you say that?"

"Cause you're the jack-off," Krush said furiously. "How can you do this to Touch? Especially now."

"It's complicated," Famous mumbled.

"Fuck you, Famous. Grow up. She's taken, so stay away."

"What if I can't?"

"Force yourself, little bro', force yourself."

"I'm trying."

"No. You're not."

"You don't—"

"I'm on my way back to town," Krush interrupted. "Dinner tonight. My hotel at seven."

"I'm not sure I can make it."

"Be there," Krush said. "We'll get into it then."

***

Money persuaded Irena to talk. One thing old Red Bentley had taught his eldest son was the power of money. Touch had always used that lesson to great advantage.

Trying not to stare at the flashing Bentley ring on the old woman's pinky, he began his line of questioning quietly at first.

"Was Sadiya your daughter?" Irena vigorously shook her head.

"It's okay if she was, Irena," he said, standing in the middle of the room because sitting didn't seem to be an option, considering there was only the unmade bed and a rickety old chair. "Nobody will do anything to you."

"I must not talk," Irena stated, mantra-style.

"Talk about what?" he pressed.

"Paulina say talking not good," Irena muttered. "Police. Immigration. She tells me to stay quiet."

"Paulina is dead."

"I know, I know," Irena wailed, her face crumpling, words tumbling from her mouth. "My baby is dead."

"I'm sorry," Touch said.

"America," Irena mumbled as if that explained everything.

"America?"

"In Russia this not happen."

Apparently, she'd never read a Russian newspaper where reports of violent crimes were rampant.

"Do you know who did this to Sadiya?" he asked.

"No, no," Irena said, shaking her head. "I know nothing. That's what I told the police. I know nothing."

At this point, Touch took out money, a thick stack of hundred-dollar bills held together with a rubber band. He didn't offer it to her, simply kept it in his hands where she could see it.

"But you do know about Draygo, don't you?" he said, watching for her reaction.

Alarm flashed across Irena's face. "Draygo? Who is Draygo?" She was obviously lying.

"No more games, Irena," Touch said, flicking several bills from the stack and handing them to her. "This stays between you and me. No police. No Immigration. Okay?"

"Okay," she agreed.

"Did Draygo kill Sadiya?"

Irena collapsed in a heap on her unmade bed, sobbing uncontrollably. "I know nothing," she cried hysterically. "Nothing!"

He peeled off a couple more bills and walked over to her. "It's good you know nothing. It's good the detectives haven't found out about Draygo." He handed her the money. "We should keep it that way."

"Yes?" she said, her tears abruptly ceasing as she grabbed the money and peered up at him.

"It's best that the memory of Sadiya is not dragged through the mud. Do you agree?"

"Oh, yes, Mr. Bentley," she said, cheering up considerably. "It is best. I tell the police nothing about men. Not their business."

"Men?" Touch questioned. "Don't you mean man? One man? Draygo?"

Irena's eyes, full of greed, slid towards the roll of bills still in his hands.

He understood immediately. Irena was telling him that there was more than one man, but that was all she was telling him. If he wanted more information, he had to pay more money.

One thing he knew for sure, Irena was definitely Sadiya's mother.

Chapter Eleven

Tristin was staying around, and Chip and the gang didn't mind at all.

"The man is crazy about you," Teddy informed her.

"The man is married," Velvet responded.

"He's still crazy about you," Teddy insisted.

"No, he's not," she said, making sure she sounded casual because she certainly didn't want anyone finding out how she really felt. "He's just looking to get laid."

"Surely he could accomplish that in New York?" Teddy pointed out, fiddling with her hair extensions during an afternoon break.

"I'm sure he can, but not with me."

"He's gorgeous!" Quinn raved, joining in. "Very urban and masculine and street. I get off on that tough, manly quality."

"Then maybe you should sleep with him," Velvet said drily.

"I wish!" Quinn responded. "I think he doesn't stroll the same boulevard as little old me."

Velvet couldn't help smiling. Not only were Teddy and Quinn off the chain, but Chip's photographs were turning out to be sensational, and the work was fun. There was also the added bonus of Tristin's presence and, much as she fought her feelings for him, she couldn't help liking him more every time she saw him.

The night before, he charmed everyone at the restaurant, followed by the walk on the beach, which, whether she cared to admit it or not, had been magical. And, after a shaky start, he'd even become friends with Tony A.

They'd all sat in the hotel lobby swapping stories until two a.m., when she'd excused herself and gone up to bed, leaving Tristin, Tony, and even Hector having a fine old time.

Wednesday morning, she was up at six, after a scant amount of sleep, and as her "team" prepared her for the day's shoot, they began plying her with questions about Tristin.

"Do you like him? What's he doing here? How long is he staying?"

"Do you like him? Exactly how rich is he? Did he fly to L.A. to see you? Have you been on his plane?"

"Do you like him? Have you slept with him?"

"Do you like him?"

Yes! She liked him. Only she wasn't about to admit it, so she played it cool, and when he appeared at the shoot around three p.m., she pretended she wasn't interested in what he'd been doing all day, although she couldn't help wondering if he had a hot little honey stashed in Beverly Hills just like Parker. And since she wasn't jumping into bed with him, was he casting his eyes around for other opportunities? There were certainly plenty of good-looking women in L.A. She'd noticed them driving up to the hotel in their Mercedes, Beamers, and their husbands' Hummers. They were all fresh and glowing, with perfectly coiffed blonde hair, immaculate manicures, toned bodies, and lightly tanned skin.

Tristin didn't so much as glance in their direction. He informed anyone who cared to listen that he'd slept until one, took a steam, and then gone shopping.

"Buy anything fab?" Teddy asked. "Anything leather?"

"Maybe," Tristin replied, looking very L.A. in a white T-shirt and white pants, the usual Nikes, mirrored shades, and plenty of bling. "I'll let you know."

Velvet admired the way he treated everyone the same. No star trips for Tristin Juzang. He was a man of the people.

She wondered what his wife thought he was doing in L.A. Did they speak on the phone every day? Did they miss each other? Or wasn't it that kind of close relationship?

Tristin watched her for a while, standing silently in the background on the beach while she did her thing.

Today it was bikini time, if you could call the two flimsy strips of leather a bikini. She was starting to feel pretty confident. It was difficult not to with all the encouragement she was getting. Chip kept up a constant stream of compliments while Teddy and Quinn creamed over the pics. Even the stoic Uma managed to throw a few nice remarks her way.

Everything was amazing. The hotel, the people she was working with, Tristin turning up in L.A. with Parker, bumping into Tony, who'd left for Chicago early that morning. It was all such an adventure.

At the next break, Tristin informed her he was going back to the hotel for a massage. "Dinner," he said in a low, commanding voice. "Tonight. Just you and me."

He wasn't asking her. He was telling her. She shivered. It was usually she who called the shots in a relationship. None of that with Tristin, he was a take-charge kind of guy, and she had to admit it made a refreshing change.

"Where's Parker?" she ventured.

"He had to get back."

"But—"

"Now, don't go fretting about it, babe. Parker's anxious to work with you. You'll meet up with him next week in New York. This trip was for him to get a feel for you."

"Do you think he liked me?" she asked, knowing that she sounded like an anxious little kid, but she was unable to help herself.

"What's not to like?" Tristin answered smoothly. "Oh, yeah, and did I mention that today you are looking hot?"

"I bet you say that to all the girls you want to go to bed with," she teased.

"Yeah, well, only the difficult ones," he responded, adjusting his cool Versace shades. "See ya later, babe."

And he strolled off. No entourage. No bodyguards. Just a simple hip-hop mogul with a yen to get into her pants.

***

Later, dinner at Mr. Chow's, a famous Beverly Hills restaurant peppered with stars, all of whom Tristin seemed to know. Outside the restaurant, several paparazzi jumped forward and took their photograph, and then they clamored for her name.

"Meet Velvet, guys," Tristin said, not at all worried about being photographed with her. "You'll all be buying this young lady's new CD soon enough."

Once they were settled at a table, Tristin leaned over, took her hand, and said, "Here's what you gotta know. It's never too early to get the hype going. By the time your CD drops, everyone will recognize your name."

"Including Toshi?" she asked, unable to prevent the words from coming out of her mouth.

"Now, why are you into spoiling a perfect night?" he said, his expression quizzical.

"Because if I was your wife and I saw your photograph with another woman, I'd be pissed."

"I'll remember that for when we're married." Had he just said that? Was she hearing things?

He ordered her a lychee martini and a selection of the most delicious food she'd ever tasted. Spareribs and seaweed, chicken satay, and duck pancakes were a few things gracing her tastebuds. It was an incredible array of dishes.

After a while, she realized she was eating too much. Tristin was watching her with an indulgent smile on his handsome face.

"Guess I was hungry," she said, trying not to stare at Catherine Zeta-Jones and Michael Douglas, who was being seated at the next table. "That's okay," Tristin said easily. "I like a girl with a big appetite."

"When are you leaving?" she asked, taking a sip of her drink.

"Whenever you're ready." Then a beat later, he continued, "I know what you meant," he said, leaning back.

"So?"

"So, like I said, whenever you're ready."

***

They were interrupted by a buxom blonde with huge fake tits and an enhanced-lip smile. She pounced on Tristin as if he was a particularly delicious item on the menu.

"How are you?" she gushed, leaning over to give him a wet kiss and an excellent view of her fake tits hanging out of a skimpy orange dress.

"I'm good," he said, coolly polite.

"How's Tash?" the blonde asked, shooting a meaningful look at Velvet. "I didn't mean tonight. I meant, when are you leaving L.A.?"

"She's good too."

An awkward silence. Fake tits waited to be introduced to Velvet. It didn't happen.

"Who was that?" Velvet asked when the blonde finally got the hint and moved on.

"Would you believe me if I told you that I got no clue?"

"Yes, I'd believe you. She's hardly your type."

"Oh," he said, grinning. "You think I have a type?"

"Well, don't you?"

"Yeah, you."

After dinner, Tristin was into club-hopping. "Need to hear what the DJs are playing," he explained. "Gotta keep my ear current."

They stopped by several clubs. He didn't dance, hardly drank, just sat back, and watched the action, and there was plenty of that going on. Settled in a booth in one of the VIP rooms, Velvet observed a pretty teenage TV queen snorting a line of coke, a well-known male movie star necking with another well-known and very married male movie star, a couple of stoned, so-called It girls hoping to score a date, and a very lonely-looking big-time female star of forty-five, pretending to be twenty-five–or at least acting as if she was.

Like Tristin, Velvet was more an observer than a doer. She was feeling great sitting next to him, taking it all in, trying to remember every single detail so that she could regale Malshonda with her adventures.

With Tristin, she was the most comfortable she'd ever felt with a man. Yes, he wanted to sleep with her, but he wasn't all over her groping and pawing, going for a quick feel. He was a real man, laid-back and unbelievably hot, and the more time she spent with him, the more she was tempted.

Once again, she started thinking, So what if he's married? If it doesn't bother him, why should it bother me?

"Guess I'd better get you to bed, your bed," Tristin said, finally winding down. "Thanks for coming with me tonight, LL. It was time for me to check out the L.A. scene."

"So that's why you came to L.A."

"No, babe," he said, giving her a long, lingering look. "You know why I came to L.A."

They made it into the limo, Tristin ignoring the attention of even more paparazzi darting around them, taking random shots.

Guess he's used to all this attention, Velvet thought. Like P. Diddy, he kind of goes with it.

"So, LL," Tristin said, leaning back against the leather seat, "what time will you finish tomorrow?"

"They've got me booked on a nine o'clock night-time flight to New York."

"Tell them to cancel it."

"Excuse me?"

"I'm full of this crazy yen to take you to Cabo," he said, giving her the look she found so irresistible.

"Cabo?" she questioned.

"Cabo San Lucas. It's this happening resort in Mexico. Why we gotta rush back to New York when we can fly there in two hours, spend the weekend, then come back to the city on Sunday? Sounds cool?"

"Amazing," she replied. "Only I can't do it."

"And that would be because...?"

"There's a lot of reasons."

"Tell me the big one, and Tristin will solve it," he said confidently.

"Well..." she began.

"Yeah," he groaned. "I know, I know. I'm married, right?"

"You said it."

"That's not such a big deal, you know."

"To you, it's not."

"No shit."

"And what if I don't want to fly to Cabo with you?" she said, testing him.

"That ain't gonna happen."

"No?"

"No."

Tristin Juzang was a difficult man to refuse. Just one look, and she was hooked. "We'll see," she said, keeping it vague.

"We'll see, the girl says." He laughed, rolling his eyes.

"Like, you think every girl says yes to you, Mr. Unturndownable?"

"Something like that," he said, grinning.

"Your ego is huge."

"Believe me, baby, that's not all."

"Tristin!"

"Move closer, LL. One kiss ain't gonna kill ya."

And so, they'd started kissing again, and it was so damn hot that she'd almost forgotten he was married.

Not quite. When the limo pulled up to the hotel, she jumped out hurriedly. "I can't do this," she said, then rushed inside and made it to the safety of her room before she weakened and changed her mind.

God! She was so confused. Her resolve was crumbling. If she went to Cabo with him, she'd be just another girl he'd screwed outside his marriage, and then what?

Before she could give it any more thought, her mom was on the phone. "Why haven't you called me back?" Fatima demanded. "I need to talk to you."

"I was out, Mama."

"I left messages."

"I know, but I thought it was too late in New York to call you. Isn't it like four in the morning there? How come you're still up?"

"What time will you be back here tomorrow?" Fatima asked tensely.

"Uh…" Velvet replied, hesitating for a moment. "I've kind of been invited to stay with some friends in Mexico."

"No!" Fatima sounded distraught. "You can't go."

"I'm not actually asking permission," Velvet retorted. "The reason I'm telling you is so you don't start imagining I've been kidnapped into a life of slavery."

Fatima gave a long-drawn-out sigh. "There's something I have to tell you, Velvet."

"Then tell me, I'm listening."

"Not over the phone."

"Why not?"

"It's something I have to tell you to your face."

"Oh, for God's sake," Velvet exploded, full of frustration. "I'm sick of this. First, you tell me nothing at all, and now that I'm out on my own enjoying myself, you can't wait to make me crazy. What is it you have to say?"

"Get back to New York as quickly as possible, Velvet, I'm begging you."

"What's so damn important?"

"Come back and find out for yourself. I promise you; it'll change your life."

Chapter Twelve

Irena fixed Touch a mug of murky dark brown tea so strong he thought he might regurgitate the foul liquid on the spot. Then she indicated that he should sit, so he balanced gingerly on the one rickety chair.

Irena settled herself on the edge of her unmade bed and proceeded to talk. Words came pouring out of her mouth, harsh words mixed with venom about her deceased daughter. "Paulina, she was always a user," Irena spat. "Always wanted the best. Daddy's little favorite."

"Where is your husband?" Touch asked. Early on in their relationship, Sadiya had informed him that both her parents had perished in a train wreck when she was an infant. Like everything else about Sadiya, that had been a lie too.

"Dead," Irena stated, clutching her own mug of tea. "Shot in Moscow thirty years ago. Not a nice man. Paulina takes after him."

"But she sent for you, brought you to America, didn't she?"

"Ha!" Irena snorted. "To be her slave. Iron her clothes. Press them. Take them to the dry cleaners. Polish her shoes. Wash her dirty underwear. Keep her secrets. I am a slave. She lives in a palace. Look where I sleep."

Touch nodded. Irena wasn't wrong. "Tell me about the men," he said. "Was she seeing Draygo while she was married to me?"

"Draygo," Irena said scornfully. "He's nothing. He is a peasant. Paulina plays with him like a toy."

"Go on," Touch encouraged.

"Paulina loved herself. Then Alex. But Alex only for sex."

"Alex?" Touch questioned.

"Boyfriend."

"Boyfriend when?"

"When she needs sex. Or money." A crafty pause. "Alex give her cash."

Did that explain the cash he'd found stuffed into her box? That would be some generous boyfriend.

"Who is Alex?"

"Bad man," Irena said, her face darkening. "Gangster. Criminal. He carries a gun."

Jesus! Sadiya certainly had led a double life.

"What's Alex's surname?" he asked, thinking that Alex might be listed in her phone book.

Irena shrugged. "Russian man," she said vaguely as if that explained everything.

"Was she seeing him when she was married to me?"

"Maybe," Irena answered cautiously.

Touch wondered if Alex had stabbed Sadiya to death, not Draygo. Was that possible?

No. Draygo was guilty. He was sure of it.

And then Sadiya's words came back to haunt him. The night she'd called him to her apartment claiming Camryn was sick, the night he'd said, "She's my daughter, isn't she." He'd said it as a statement, not a question.

But Sadiya had murmured a sly, "Maybe," and now, in view of what Irena was telling him, there was a distinct possibility that Camryn might not be his child. She could be Draygo's or even Alex's. He felt sick.

"I give police nothing," Irena said, pursing her lips. "You tell them what I say, I deny." She stood up and snatched the mug out of his hand. "You no like tea?" she said accusingly. "Not strong enough?"

"It's a little too strong."

"I know who murdered Paulina," she said, just like that.

A chill pervaded his body. "Who?"

Another crafty expression crossed her weather-beaten face. "You have Paulina's box? Her money?"

"I just gave you—"

"You want to know who stabbed her?" Irena said flatly, "Come back, bring me the box. It should be mine."

"What makes you think I have it?"

"Someone took it from the apartment. I think it's you."

"And if it wasn't me?"

"Then our talk is finished."

***

"Hi, Grams," Shemika said, arriving unannounced at her grandmother's hotel apartment.

"What are you doing here?" Grandma Poppy asked, shushing her two dogs, who were running around in circles, barking.

"I came to tell you we're postponing the wedding."

"I heard," Grandma Poppy said, calming her yapping dogs with a commanding gesture. "Your mother phoned me. In lieu of the terrible event that has taken place, a postponement is the correct thing to do."

"Mom seems to think so," Shemika said. "She's livid because my name has been dragged into the newspapers."

"I'm sure she is."

"She wants me to break off my engagement, give Touch back his ring, quit my job, and leave the country," Shemika continued, pulling up a chair.

"Ah," Grandma Poppy sighed. "Nancy. Overreacting as usual." A pause. "And how do you feel about breaking your engagement to Touch?"

"Here's the thing, Grams, I, uh, have another problem that's even worse."

"What could possibly be worse than your overly dramatic mother trying to tell you what to do?" Grandma Poppy inquired, tapping her elegant long fingers on the table beside her.

"You're so wise, Grams," Shemika said. "That's why I came here." She glanced at Hueng, hovering near the door.

Grandma Poppy followed her eyes. "Hueng," she said, raising her voice and waving a hand imperiously, "out, my granddaughter has private things to tell me. Go now." Hueng made a rapid exit. "What is it, dear girl? Speak up."

"Well..." Shemika said hesitantly. "It's something my mother couldn't possibly understand. I'm not even sure you will."

"Try me, dear."

"I, I did something foolish," Shemika stammered, "and now I don't know how to handle the situation."

"Go ahead."

"Remember I told you about my bachelorette night?"

"You'd better remind me. My memory's not what it used to be."

"We had, you know, drinks and fun and male strippers."

"Ooh, male strippers," Grandma Poppy said, eyes gleaming as she clapped her hands together. "What a pity we didn't have those when I was young."

"Anyway, it got kind of crazy."

"Nothing wrong with a young girl getting crazy."

"Only I got a little too crazy," Shemika admitted.

"What happened?"

"I slept with a stranger," Shemika blurted out. "I didn't know his name or anything about him, and he didn't know who I was. It was just one of those unbelievable things."

"I presume you regret it?" Grandma Poppy said, not appearing to be at all shocked.

"Yes, I mean, no," Shemika muttered, totally flustered. "You see, it turns out he's someone I know."

"I'm sure you do know him if you went to bed with him."

"It's bad, Grams." A long silent beat. "He's Touch's brother."

"Excuse me?"

"Touch's younger brother, Famous. You met him at the rehearsal dinner. He was at your table with the Italian model you thought was so charming. She's kind of his girlfriend."

"I'm a tad confused," Grandma Poppy said. "You slept with a man whom you didn't know, and he didn't know you. Yet you have a fiancé, and he has a girlfriend. Am I correct?"

"Yes, that's exactly it."

"Have you told Touch?"

"No, I feel too guilty. I want to tell him, but I just can't."

"That's good because you have to keep this to yourself."

"I do?"

"Yes," Grandma Poppy said firmly, "you most certainly do. Telling Touch will only create bigger problems."

"I have a bigger problem already. I want to be with Famous, and yet I know, especially in view of what's going on, that I must stay with Touch."

"And does Famous feel the same way?"

"Yes."

"What about the Italian girl?"

"She's not his steady girlfriend. He's breaking up with her so that he can be with me."

"Men always say that," Grandma Poppy mused, a faraway look in her eyes. "They're always after the nooky they can't have."

"Grandma! Where did you learn words like "nooky"?"

"I'm telling you the truth, dear. It's best that you hear it from me."

"I need your advice, Grams," Shemika said, beginning to feel slightly desperate. "You're smart, you've been around the world, and you've experienced a wonderful marriage, so please tell me what I should do."

"This will sound very old-fashioned," Grandma Poppy said, scooping up one of her dogs and petting the furry creature.

"I don't care."

"Well, if Famous is the man for you, then you must follow your heart, dear, follow your heart. Otherwise, you could spend the rest of your life regretting it."

***

His mind churning with a hundred different thoughts, Touch drove home from Brighton Beach to the sanctuary of his apartment.

Sadiya's life was turning out to have been much more complicated than even he could have imagined. First, there was Draygo, who'd probably been splitting the blackmail money with her. Now he'd found out about Alex, and who the hell was he?

The thought occurred to him once more, had she been sleeping with this Alex when they were married? Was she fucking another man while they were together? Was Alex Camryn's father?

Would Sadiya have stooped that low?

Yes, Sadiya had been capable of anything.

Fury began to build within him. A fury so white-hot, he almost ran his car off the road.

Sadiya had always been into sex, much more so than he. She'd often suggested threesomes and handcuffs and leather fetishes. He'd turned down all her suggestions, put off by what he considered her kinky desires.

After the birth of Camryn, they'd very rarely had sex at all. Was it then that she'd turned to Alex for the sex she craved? Or had she been sleeping with him before?

Damn the woman. He couldn't even confront her. She was dead. Murdered. And according to her loving mother, the killer was out there, and Irena knew who it was.

How should he handle this? Hand over Sadiya's box to Irena, money and all? Or give it to the detectives?

He was torn. If the killer wasn't Draygo, what did he care?

Of course, he cared. Sadiya had been brutally murdered, and however he felt about her, it was a terrible act of violence.

Several messages were waiting for him at home. One was from Mrs. Conner in Montauk, saying that Camryn was fine and having a lovely time. She had even put Camryn on the phone to say good night. Next, there was an abrupt message from Red, requesting his presence at a ten a.m. meeting the next day, no mention of Sadiya's demise. Did the old man think he could summon these meetings at random, and everyone would come running? It was such a joke.

The third message was from Krush, still in town at the Four Seasons, requesting that Touch join him and Famous for dinner. The last thing he felt like doing was sitting down for dinner with his brothers. He didn't feel like seeing anyone, including Shemika. He had too much on his mind.

Fifteen minutes later, the desk clerk buzzed up to inform him that Detective Banks was downstairs.

Jesus Christ! Was the annoying detective ever going to leave him alone? Now, what was he supposed to do?

"Send him up," he said, thinking he'd get rid of him fast.

A few minutes later, Detective Banks lumbered into the foyer of his apartment. This time he was alone.

"This is getting to be a habit," Touch said abruptly. "And it's not a habit I care to keep cultivating."

"Sorry to bother you, Mr. Bentley," Detective Banks said. "I have a couple of very quick questions to ask you. We're making progress, and there are a few things you might be able to help me out with."

"Yes?" Touch said, keeping the detective standing in the foyer, determined not to invite him in.

"According to the doorman at the ex-Mrs. Bentley's apartment, she entertained several male visitors on a regular basis. Did you happen to know this?"

"I told you," Touch said. "I had no idea who she was seeing after we separated."

"I thought you might be able to give me names."

"Now, why would I be able to do that?"

"Just a thought, Mr. Bentley."

"Look," Touch said, attempting to keep his temper under wraps, "in the future, kindly contact me through my lawyer. You cannot keep turning up at my apartment whenever you feel like it."

"I was under the impression you'd be anxious to get this case cleared up as quickly as possible," Detective Banks said, pushing his glasses up the bridge of his nose. "I'm getting calls from the captain. He's getting calls from downtown. It's becoming a very big deal."

"I would imagine a woman being murdered in her own bed in the heart of Manhattan is a big deal," Touch said.

"Perhaps if I gave you some descriptions, you'd be able to help me."

"No," Touch said sharply. "I wouldn't."

"Were you aware that she had three regular male visitors?"

Touch thought quickly. One must be Draygo; obviously, one was Alex, but who was the third?

He shook his head. "Talk to her mother again, and maybe she can help you. I certainly can't."

"Have you spoken to Irena?" Detective Banks asked, stroking his mustache.

Hmm…a direct question. Should he lie and say no? Or should he admit that he'd gone to visit Irena in Brighton Beach? "You pointed out that if she was Sadiya's mother, it would make her my child's grandmother. So, yes, I did go see her."

"Really?" the detective said, still stroking his mustache. "And what did she have to say?"

"Nothing that she hasn't already said to you."

The detective gave him a long, brooding stare. "You might be interested to know that we're putting together new evidence all the time."

"What kind of evidence?"

"DNA samples are being tested, hair, skin." Another long beat. "You know, murderers never understand how they get caught. The truth is, they get caught because they're careless. They think a pair of gloves will do it. Not anymore."

"Are we done, Detective?" Touch asked impatiently.

"For now."

Touch flung open the front door, and Detective Banks stepped outside. "I'll keep you informed, Mr. Bentley," he said.

"Do that," Touch said, slamming the door and frowning. His main concern was Draygo, and if Draygo hadn't killed her, could it have been Alex? And who was the third man? He needed to find out.

***

Famous didn't relish the thought of having dinner with Krush; he wanted to be with Shemika. Nevertheless, when he called her and told her he was coming over, she gave him a speech about how she needed time and space to work out what she was going to do.

This alarmed him. He'd just broken up with his long-time girlfriend, and now Shemika was backing off. What kind of crap was that?

Then to disturb him further, his mother called. "What the hell's going on with that damn family?" Sukari slurred, wasted, and belligerent. "I told you to stay away from the bastards. I warned you."

"Hey, listen, Mom—"

"No. You damn well listen to me. They're degenerates, all of them. You stay the hell away, Famous. I mean it."

He got her off the phone as quickly as possible. Then, to calm his nerves, he decided he needed a drink, one small shot of vodka.

What harm was there in one shot of vodka?

After a quick search of the apartment, he discovered a half-full bottle of Grey Goose nestled in Eddie's kitchen cupboard. One drink after almost three years of sobriety. He could handle it. Right on, he could handle it.

***

I'm in limbo, Shemika thought. I'm confused and unhappy and filled with guilt. Maybe my mother is right. Maybe I should get out of town.

She'd made up her mind not to see Famous again until she'd come to a decision about Touch. What should she do? Tell Touch they were over, then start seeing his brother? How right was that?

128

Grandma Poppy had told her to follow her heart, and what did her heart say? She didn't know. She wasn't sure.

And while she was having these thoughts, it occurred to her that lately, Touch seemed to have become very distant, making no attempt to see her. She understood why, with all that he was going through, but surely, if they were really close, he would want her to be with him at a time like this.

On her way home, she decided to visit Megan in the hospital, hoping they'd have a chance to talk.

When she walked into Megan's hospital room, Tyrese was already there, and so were Megan's parents.

"Hi!" Megan said, delighted to see her. "We're going home tomorrow. Isn't that great?"

The baby was thriving, and Megan was glowing, with no sign of postpartum blues. "I'm itching to get out of here," Megan said excitedly. "Isn't he the cutest?"

Shemika agreed that, yes, indeed Tyrese Junior was the cutest, and she sat there for a while, feeling out of place and anxious to leave. Close as she was to Megan, it was a family event.

After a polite half-hour, she excused herself, hurried home, and continued to mull over her situation.

There didn't seem to be an answer in sight.

***

"Her fucking people are driving my fucking people fucking loco!" The unmistakable voice of Patrick Sumter.

"Listen to me, Patrick. I'm Chilly's lawyer," Krush said evenly. "I don't get into those kinds of details. Tell them to contact her publicist or one of her assistants."

"Fucking pink. She wants everything fucking pink," Patrick complained. "She's a whack-job. She's even asked for the water in the pool to be tinted pink!"

"Did you hear me, Patrick?"

"Yeah, yeah, I heard you." A long beat and a change of tone. "Where's my fucking money?"

"You'll have it this weekend," Krush assured him. "In cash, just the way you wanted."

"About time," Patrick grumbled.

Krush hung up. Since staying with Touch was not on his agenda, he'd checked back into the Four Seasons. Comfortable as Touch's apartment was, he preferred the freedom of a hotel. Besides, after the meeting with Red, he planned on flying back to L.A. No more delays. He'd been away almost a week, much longer than he'd anticipated.

He couldn't reach Touch anyway. His brother wasn't at his office, and there was no answer on his cell, so he left a message about dinner.

He hoped that by this time, Touch had handed Sadiya's box and everything in it over to the detectives. If he hadn't, he was a fool.

The news stations were still all over Sadiya's murder. It was as if they had nothing else to cover. And yet all Krush could think about were Red's ominous words concerning his mother's death.

Tomorrow he'd get to the real truth. That's if Red was capable of telling the truth. And that was doubtful, very doubtful.

***

"Lady Bentley knows," Fatima said, standing in the library.

Sprawled on the leather couch, newspapers scattered around him, Red gave her a canny look. "What does the bitch know?"

"About Velvet," Fatima said wearily. "You promised me nobody would ever find out."

"Promises mean nothing," Red said roughly. "You're smart enough to realize that."

"What are you going to do?"

"You'll see, along with all of them. I want you in the meeting I'm having tomorrow morning. I want Velvet there too."

"That's not possible. She's in Los Angeles."

"Get her back."

"I'll try."

"Don't try," he said roughly. "Do it!"

***

After Detective Banks left, Touch wished he'd given him the box and stepped away, as Krush had suggested. But he couldn't do it. The information in the box would eventually lead them to Draygo, and the truth that Sadiya had been a bigamist would be revealed.

And where would that leave him and Camryn? The illegitimate child and the husband who never was. The fool who'd married a Russian ex-hooker who had still been married to another man.

He simply couldn't do it. Not to his Camryn. Not to the light of his life.

He made a sudden decision to take the box to Irena. She'd never give it to the police. He'd hide it away and make good use of the money.

Yes. That was the answer. He'd take it to her tonight, get it over with.

Fearing he'd change his mind, he picked up the phone and called her.

She answered with a raspy voice.

"Irena," he said. "It's Mr. Bentley. About that matter, we discussed. I'm bringing you what you requested on the condition you mention nothing about Draygo or the other men to the police. Do we have an agreement?"

"When you come?" she asked. He could almost imagine her rubbing her hands together in anticipation of the riches she was about to inherit.

"I'll be there in an hour. And I expect you to tell me everything you know."

Just as he was leaving the apartment, Krush phoned. "Dinner with me and Famous," Krush said. "I left you a message."

"Not tonight," he replied abruptly. "Maybe tomorrow. I'll be in L.A. tomorrow."

"Then we'll have lunch before you leave, after the meeting with Red."

"You'll be at the meeting?" Krush asked.

"If you and Famous are going, I'll be there. What do you think that dumb old bastard wants now?"

"When I spoke to him on the phone, he mumbled something about my mother."

"Your mother?" Touch said, frowning.

"Why do you think I turned around and came back? I was almost at the airport when he called."

"What did he say?"

"He intimated that her death was due to more than just a plane crash."

"That's ridiculous."

"Is it?" Krush said slowly. "Do you ever think about your mother's death?"

"Well, of course, I do. But you're not saying—"

"Hey, I don't know what I'm saying. It's Red Bentley we're dealing with, so consider the man and what he's capable of."

Touch hung up the phone and slumped into a deep depression. All his life, he'd wondered about his mother's untimely death. Pamela was an exquisite twenty-six-year-old woman who'd died in her sleep six months after giving birth to him. The official word was heart failure, and when, at the age of thirteen, Touch had started asking questions, Red had told him that his mother had always suffered from a defective heart and that he was never to mention her again.

The only way Touch knew his mother was through the few photographs he had been able to find of her. Pamela. His mother. Dark hair. Huge eyes. A Madonna-like smile.

He missed knowing her with a deep wrenching hurt in his gut. And if Red was in any way responsible for her death…

It was a thought he almost couldn't face.

Von Diesel

Chapter Twelve

The tabloids were due to hit the street on Thursday, so Red Bentley had copies, straight off the press, delivered to his house Wednesday night. The headlines were scandalous.

The Bentley Dynasty!

Ex-Model Stabbed to Death!

Billionaire Media Tycoon Red Bentley's Family Secrets That Led to Sex, Drugs, and Murder!

Wild Days of the Bentley Brothers!

Murder in Manhattan!

Beautiful Society Woman Slain!

Who Killed Sadiya?

Truth and Fact, the most scurrilous rag of all, had unearthed plenty. Sadiya, the beautiful murder victim, was the only one spared, although they'd managed to dig up several semi-nude pin-up photos of her, taken when she'd first arrived in America and had apparently harbored hopes of being a model.

Touchwell Bentley was portrayed as a business-obsessed, real-estate tycoon with a much younger fiancee who was due to inherit millions when her rich society grandmother passed. The implication being that Touch had divorced Sadiya to get his hands on Shemika's inheritance. There were pictures of Touch and Shemika taken at their rehearsal dinner and a large photo of Touch, Sadiya, and Camryn on a skiing vacation when Camryn was three.

Krush Bentley was written about as a playboy Hollywood lawyer with gambling connections to Vegas and the Mob. There were photos of him with Chilly Rose and several ex-girlfriends, including Clarissa Duboy. The article even insinuated that the emancipation of Chilly Rose had been brokered by Krush so that he could get a large cut of her money and as many nights as he wanted with the teenage pop diva.

Famous came off worst of all. Along with several bare-chested modeling shots taken when he'd first arrived in Milan, there were photographs of him from his wild New York days, falling down drunk at various clubs and parties, mostly with girls in barely-there dresses who looked like underage hookers.

Red Bentley was featured heavily. The billionaire patriarch of the family was a tempting target. Diligent journalists had no trouble digging up a wealth of information, including his many wives, their unfortunate deaths, the scandalous divorce and subsequent affair with Lady J Bentley, and numerous business machinations, including a slew of hostile takeovers and fraught relationships with other media moguls who considered themselves his peers.

Red Bentley was an old-fashioned, ego-driven, megalomaniac, and the rags relished the chance of putting their investigative skills to work, especially *Truth and Fact*, which happened to come under the umbrella of a host of publications owned by one of Red's archrivals, of which, over the years, he'd had quite a few.

When Red saw the tabloids, particularly Truth and Fact, he went berserk, stamping around his house in a frenzied fury, shouting and yelling obscenities. The entire household heard him, Lady J Bentley, sequestered in her room, Fatima, who'd been hoping for another chance to speak with him privately, the cook, the laundress, the maids.

"Fuck the dirty, lying, cocksucking bastards!' he screamed. "Fuck Sadiya, that Russian cunt! And fuck the stupid boys I should never have allowed my dumb fucking wives to bring into this world!"

After venting for a while, he made a call, summoned his driver, and stomped out of the house.

Nobody cared to deal with Red Bentley when he'd worked himself up into one of his turbulent frenzies.

Von Diesel

Chapter Thirteen

Famous turned up for dinner an hour late and totally wasted. Watching him weave his way towards the table, Krush groaned inwardly. With all that was going on, Famous had to choose this moment to slide out of sobriety and turn into the drunk he used to be.

"Sorry I'm late," Famous slurred as he arrived at the table. "Had to go see my mom."

"Sukari's in town?" Krush questioned, wondering if mother and son had been out on a drinking binge together.

"Kinda. Sorta," Famous said, attempting to pull out a chair and almost losing his balance. "You know Sukari; she had me trapped on the phone."

Krush realized there was no sense in pretending he didn't know what was going on. That would just be a monumental waste of time. "Okay," he said, trying not to sound too judgmental. "What made you do it?"

"Huh?" Famous said blankly. "Do what?"

"Take a drink."

"Are you fucking shitting me?" Famous said, managing to look outraged. "You know I'm in the goddamn program."

"Yes, I'm aware of that," Krush answered calmly. "And exactly when did you last attend a meeting?"

"A meeting," Famous mumbled. "Ah...let me see. A meeting..." His eyes glazed over. "Who am I meeting?"

Krush clicked his fingers for the check. "I'm taking you upstairs."

"Why are we doing that?" Famous grumbled. "I gotta eat, gotta call my girl." His voice started getting louder. "Gotta call my goddamn girl." Without warning, he was on his feet, swaying and shouting. "Shemika. Where the fuck are ya? Shemika, baby. Shemika, bitch!"

Other patrons turned to stare.

Jumping up, Krush grabbed his brother's arm in a vice-like grip. "We're outta here," he said, steering him towards the entrance. "Do not say another word."

***

Before Isha had a chance to contact Red Bentley, Inka phoned.

"He wants us," Inka stated, sounding quite pleased with herself.

"Who wants us?" Isha asked. After her long night of rough sex with Alex Pinchinoff, she wasn't in the mood for new action, even if it meant big bucks.

"The old guy, of course," Inka said triumphantly. "I knew he couldn't resist."

"Red Bentley?" Isha questioned. If it was Red, how convenient was that?

"Mr. Viagra himself," Inka said with a brittle laugh. "The old man sounded agitated. I tell him two thousand apiece, double we stay all night."

"He agreed?"

"Bring rubber handcuffs and special lotion. I run out. I had an important client from the UN. He wants lotion head to toe, especially around his balls. No sex, just lotion." She gave another brittle laugh. "Asshole."

"They're all assholes," Isha said.

"Where you been?" Inka asked.

"Alex Pinchinoff."

"Ah, the dangerous one."

"Dangerous and sexy."

"You don't get enough at work?"

"It make change."

"I call for cab. You want I pick you up?"

"How soon?"

"Fifteen minutes."

"I'll be downstairs."

This couldn't have worked out better. Now she could blackmail Red to his face. Well, maybe not blackmail. That was too harsh a word. Merely allow him an opportunity to pay to have certain information suppressed.

But what about Inka? She couldn't do it in front of her. Damn! She'd have to figure something out.

***

Driving into a certain area of Brighton Beach at night was scary. The restaurants and nightclubs were lit up while noisy and half-drunk patrons spilled out onto the sidewalk.

Searching for a parking spot, Touch became very aware that he was carrying a box, which he'd put inside a canvas bag, then locked into the trunk, a box that contained half a million bucks in cash, plus a few priceless gemstones. The only items he removed from it were Sadiya's address book, filled with the numbers of all her Russian acquaintances, along with her birth certificate and marriage certificate to Draygo. The moment he got home, he would burn them, burn away all traces of her duplicitous past.

Damnit, he was turning into a criminal, planning to destroy what could turn out to be very valuable evidence in a murder case. Shades of Red Bentley. It was the kind of thing Red would do without a second thought.

He didn't want to become like his father, but all rational thought seemed to have deserted him. He was convinced that this was something he had to do to protect his daughter if, indeed, Camryn was his daughter. The thought that she might not be paralyzed him. She was all he had, her and Shemika.

A green Buick conveniently slid out of a parking spot. Touch backed his Mercedes into the vacant space, bumping the fender of an old Cadillac parked behind.

Almost immediately, a man emerged from the Cadillac, zipping up his fly. "What's wrong with you?" the man yelled. He was big, bald, and bad-tempered. "You need a fucking compass to park your shitty German car?"

Touch got out of his Mercedes. "Sorry," he muttered. The last thing he wanted was a scene. "I don't think there's any damage."

"You don't, huh?" the man sneered belligerently. "That's where you and I differ, my friend. Take a look at my bumper! There's a couple hundred bucks worth of damage."

Touch attempted to peer at the supposedly damaged car. It was too dark to see anything.

A young girl emerged from the Cadillac, young enough to be the bald man's daughter, although she obviously wasn't. Her clothes were askew, and her lipstick smudged across her chin.

"Here's my witness," the man said triumphantly.

"Where's my twenty?" the girl demanded in a tiny voice, pulling on his sleeve.

"Shut up," the man hissed, glaring at her. "You'll get your money. We're not finished."

Touch got the picture. "Will two hundred cover it?" he asked.

The bald man thought about it for a nano-second. "Make it two-fifty, and I won't bother calling the cops to report an accident," he said, adjusting his crotch.

"Right," Touch said. He hated giving in to this oaf's extortion, but anything to avoid more of a confrontation. Turning away from the man, he pulled out his wallet, extracted the right amount of money, then handed it over.

The bald man shoved the bills into his pocket and said, "What you down here looking for? Maybe I can help you find it."

"That's all right," Touch said. "I'm visiting a relative."

"A relative, huh?"

"Are we doing it or not?" the young girl whined, tugging on the bald man's shirtsleeve.

"Yeah, we're doing it," he said, throwing Touch a lascivious wink.

The two of them got back into the Cadillac.

Touch waited a few minutes before he opened the trunk of his Mercedes. Then he quickly took out the canvas bag, crossed the street, and entered Irena's building.

***

Standing astride Red Bentley, wearing nothing but sheer black stockings, a leather garter belt, and ridiculously high stilettos, Isha thought the old man looked unusually pale. Of course, he had just indulged in a series of sexual activities with two beautiful women, activities probably far too taxing for a seventy-nine-year-old man, she'd discovered his age by reading the newspapers, and then there was the matter of the Viagra he'd been taking on what seemed a regular basis. It couldn't be healthy for a man his age.

Isha was worried about his well-being. What if he had a seizure or a heart attack? Either could turn out to be deadly, and where would that leave her and the major pay that she hoped to extract from him?

Right now, he was demanding that she handcuff and punish him. It was one of his favorite scenarios, smack his wrinkled old ass until it was rosy.

Inka was in the bathroom taking a leisurely shower, or so she said. Inka worked hard with her clients, but she claimed they never made her come, so whenever there was a break, she locked herself away and pleasured herself.

This suited Isha fine because it gave her the opportunity she was looking for. "How much you pay for Draygo story to stay quiet?" she ventured.

"What?" Red growled, staring up at the woman who stood astride him.

She wasn't supposed to talk. He didn't appreciate talkers.

"Your daughter-in-law's real husband."

"My daughter-in-law's what?"

"Legitimate husband."

He ran his gnarled hand up her thigh. "Is this part of the punishment?"

"No. This real stuff," Isha said quickly. "Sadiya no marry Touch, she already married to my friend Draygo. That makes her bigamist. Not only bigamist, in Moscow, she prostitute." Isha paused to let her words sink in. "How much you pay for story to stay quiet?"

"Are you trying to blackmail me?" Red asked incredulously, then burst into derisive laughter. "You honestly think I didn't know who Sadiya was? She was a cheap whore, like you. I understood that the moment I saw her."

"I am not cheap," Isha muttered, her dreams of scoring a fortune crashing around her.

"No, you're not," Red agreed. "Now, put your mouth where it's supposed to be and shut the fuck up."

***

The same smell of cat piss and stale beer assailed Touch's nostrils as he entered Irena's building. The question occurred to him, why had Sadiya allowed her mother to live in such squalor? Then again, it was unlikely that Sadiya had ever visited the dank apartment in Brighton Beach, so he'd give her the benefit of the doubt and assume she hadn't realized how bad it was.

He climbed the darkened stairs, clutching the bag tightly to his chest. This was so unlike anything he'd ever done before. Was he losing his mind? It was insane behavior. Krush was right. He could get himself arrested for concealing evidence.

At least by giving the box to Irena, he was no longer responsible for it. And who could prove that he'd taken it from her apartment? No one.

Halfway up the second flight of stairs, a woman in a sloppy housecoat burst out of a door yelling in a foreign language. She was being chased by a skinny runt of a man wielding a leather belt. The two of them shoved their way past Touch as if he didn't exist. He took a deep breath and made it up the rest of the stairs fast.

If Irena was smart, she'd move out of this dump tomorrow. She'd have enough money to do whatever the hell she wanted, although he should warn her not to do anything with the gemstones for a while. Who knew where they had come from? He should also tell her to take off Sadiya's diamond ring and put it away.

Then another question occurred to him, how had she got the ring? She must have stolen it, so did that mean she had been in Sadiya's apartment after she was killed? Had she taken the ring off Sadiya's lifeless finger? Or was she actually there when Sadiya was stabbed to death?

At least it was kind of poetic justice that Sadiya's money, and where it had come from, he didn't even want to think about, was going to her mother, a woman for whose welfare she'd obviously cared nothing.

He made it to Irena's apartment and knocked on the door. It swung open, and her cat darted out, hissing angrily.

The stench of burned milk hit him as he entered, calling her name.

She was sitting in the one rickety chair watching her black-and-white TV. Her back was to him. The sound of the TV was too loud, and sparks were coming from the hot plate in the corner.

"Irena," he said loudly, "something's burning." She didn't move.

"Can you turn the TV down?" he shouted.

Still no answer.

He moved in front of her.

She was dead—a single neat bullet-hole right in the center of her forehead.

Chapter Fourteen

It took him a while, but Krush finally managed to sober Famous up. After gallons of coffee, an icy cold shower, several Tylenol, and a major sweat-out in the hotel gym, Famous started groaning. How could he have done it? What was the matter with him? He was one big fucking loser.

"Shit happens," Krush assured him as they sat around in his suite. "You made a wrong move, and now it's up to you to make sure it doesn't happen again."

"I feel like such a dumb jerk." Famous groaned, pushing his hands through his hair.

"Beating yourself up won't help," Krush said. "You did it, it's over, and as soon as possible, you need to get to a meeting. It's imperative you attend on a regular basis. Plus, you've got to find a sponsor."

"I had one in Italy," Famous said, downing his fifth cup of coffee. "Any time I felt the urge, I called this guy, and he talked me down. It worked great."

"Yeah, well, what obviously does not work great is you not going to meetings," Krush pointed out.

"I get it."

"I hope so."

"Guess I wasn't thinking straight with all this stuff going on," Famous said, trying to make excuses. "You know, Kareema is leaving. Shemika, not wanting to hurt Touch."

"Like, you do?" Krush questioned.

"There's no way I want to hurt him. What I do want is to be with Shemika."

"That's what you want, huh?" Krush sighed. "You're sure?"

"Yeah, that's it."

"You got anything to offer her, little bro"? You thought about that?"

"Huh?"

"If she leaves Touch, what makes you think it'll work out between the two of you? You've no steady job, no apartment. You don't even have a car."

"Make me feel better about myself, why don't you?" Famous said wryly.

"I'm being real. Are you?"

"What do you mean by that?"

"Kareema seemed great. Beautiful, successful, fun. Could be you're making a big mistake?"

"You don't get it, Krush," Famous said earnestly. "I love Shemika, and she loves me."

"Did she tell you that?"

"No, but—"

"She didn't tell you?"

"It's early days."

"So, what's your plan?"

"We don't have one."

"Try this."

"What?"

"How about you leave her alone for a while, let her make her own decisions, then see what happens?"

"I don't think I can do that."

"Look," Krush said, the voice of reason, "force her into doing something now, and she's likely to resent you. When and if she decides to leave Touch, it has to be her move, not because you talked her into it. Then, later, if the two of you do get together…it won't be so bad for Touch."

"I suppose you could be right," Famous mumbled reluctantly.

148

"I know I am. In the meantime, I think you should fly to L.A. with me tomorrow. It'll give you a chance to get your head straight, put some space between you and this situation."

"I can't—"

"Yes, you can," Krush said forcefully. "I'm booking you a ticket, so get your ass over to your apartment and pack. I'll see you at the house of horrors in the morning. We'll take off from there."

***

Touch stumbled from Irena's apartment, his heart beating wildly. This was the second dead woman he'd seen in less than a week. What the fuck was happening to his nice orderly life?

A few days ago, he'd had everything under control, everything except his finances, and now that problem was taken care of. But his personal life was a fucking nightmare. And it was all the fault of Draygo Bushkin, the Russian prick with his threats and blackmail.

Because of Draygo, two women were dead. Somehow or other, he must have discovered that Irena was about to reveal his identity as the man who'd killed Sadiya, so he'd silenced her too. This time with a gun.

Totally panicked, Touch raced down the concrete stairs. He'd taken one look at Irena and fled, desperate to get out of her room and away from the devastating stench of death.

As he made his way rapidly down the stairs, he started going over what he'd seen. He hadn't noticed any blood, just a small, neat hole right in the middle of her forehead.

Maybe she wasn't dead. He should have felt her pulse. Although why would he touch her?

Von Diesel

Should he call the police? That was the big question.

Yes.

No!

How was he going to explain a second visit to Irena? What if they thought he had had something to do with her murder?

He had no alibi. Christ! He needed an alibi.

Shemika. He'd go straight to Shemika. Tell the police, should they ask, that he'd been with her all night.

Yes. That was a plan. He had to have a plan. Otherwise, he'd look guilty as hell. He could just imagine Detective Banks' shitty-looking face. *"Tell me, Mr. Bentley, why did you go back to visit Irena a second time? To kill her? Is that it? To stop her telling us that you murdered your wife? Sorry, Mr. Bentley, your ex-wife."*

Yes, Detective Banks would go to town on this one.

I should call my lawyer, he thought.

Why? I'm not guilty of anything. Best to keep quiet. Nobody knows I'm here. It would be foolish to open anything up.

Aren't you going to report a murder?

No. I'm not.

And as these thoughts flew around in his brain, he continued hurrying down the stairs, still clutching the canvas bag, sweating profusely, and agonizing over what to do next.

***

"I thought we would stay all night," Inka said, making a disappointed face.

"Why would I ever want to spend the night with two whores like you?" Red Bentley said, getting off the bed and starting to dress.

150

"Because you like us," Inka said, in her best girly voice. "Because we're sexy, and you like fucking us."

"Ask your friend why you're not staying," Red said, indicating Isha.

"Your blackmailing friend."

"What you say?" Inka said blankly, looking from Red to Isha.

"Didn't she tell you?" Red sneered. "Cut you in?"

Inka stared at Isha. Isha shrugged as if she had no idea what he was talking about. Damn him. If the old fart said anything, she would deny it.

"Cut me in on what?" Inka asked, at last, pouting just a little bit.

"She'll tell you," Red said, pulling on his pants. He was bored with both of them. They'd done their job, and now he wanted them gone.

He walked over to the dresser, picked up his wallet, and threw a flurry of hundred-dollar bills in their direction. "Out," he said. "Now."

***

Halfway down the stairs, Touch tripped, and, before he could save himself, he began to fall, crashing down several of the concrete stairs on his knees. The shock and pain hit him immediately, while the canvas bag shot out of his hands and plummeted over the stairwell to the ground floor.

"Shit!" he muttered, grabbing the side rail and staggering to his feet. Could this day get any worse? His pants were ripped, he could barely stand, and the pain in his right knee was excruciating.

Somehow or other, he made his way down the rest of the stairs, reaching the bag just in time as a lank-haired youth was about to scoop it up.

"That's mine," Touch said, breathing heavily.

"Says who?" the boy questioned. He was sixteen or seventeen with sallow features and a sullen attitude.

"It's mine," Touch repeated sharply. "I dropped it."

"What's in it?" the boy asked, his hand hovering near the handle.

"None of your damn business," Touch shouted, snatching up the bag and limping towards the door.

"I should get a fucking reward," the boy yelled after him.

"Bullshit," Touch muttered, crossing the street and reaching the safety of his car.

He leaned against the side of his Mercedes for a moment before he got in. Then he slid behind the wheel, placed the canvas bag on the passenger seat, and stared at it.

What was he going to do with the money and gemstones now? What the hell was he going to do?

***

Somewhere in her sleep, Shemika could hear banging, a doorbell ringing. Slowly opening her eyes, she realized the noise wasn't part of her dream. Someone was hammering at her front door.

She groped for the bedside clock and noted it was almost midnight. Now, who would be pounding at her door so late?

Famous. It had to be Famous.

For a moment, she lay very still, hoping he'd go away. But he didn't. The incessant ringing of the bell continued until she was forced to get out of bed before he woke the people in the next apartment.

She reached for a robe and made her way to the front door. "Famous," she said firmly, not opening the door. "Go away."

"It's Touch. Will you please open up?"

Oh, God! Touch had found out about her and Famous, and he was here to confront her.

For a moment, she froze, not sure what to do.

"Hurry up, Shemika," he said, raising his voice.

Had Famous told him? Confessed? Or had Krush given him the bad news?

Okay. Don't panic, she thought. I can handle this.

Taking a long, deep breath, she flung open the door. Touch stumbled inside. He looked dreadful, disheveled, and unkempt, totally unlike the Touch she knew. It was obvious that he'd taken the news badly. She wasn't surprised.

"I...I don't know what to say," she began, searching for the right words. "It wasn't planned...It, uh, just happened."

"I need to use the bathroom," he said, pushing past her. "I'll explain everything in a minute."

He hurried past into her bedroom, and then she heard her bathroom door slam.

She stood in the hallway for a moment, nonplussed. What had he meant by I'll explain everything in a minute? Wasn't she the one who was supposed to be doing the explaining?

And was it her imagination, or were his pants all ripped at the knees? And why did he look all sweaty and messed up?

Had he and Famous had a fight? That would be so bad, and she couldn't stand it.

Famous. She should call Famous and find out what had taken place. She could do it while Touch was in the bathroom.

She ran into her bedroom and picked up the phone, keeping a close eye on the bathroom door.

"Hey," Famous said, delighted to hear from her.

"What happened?" she asked in a low voice.

Famous hesitated a moment. "Look, I didn't intend to do it," he said, trying to figure out how she'd found out about his drinking. "It was just one of those things."

"It's so wrong," she said furiously.

"I'm sorry," he said. "It's not something I sat around planning to do."

"If anyone was going to tell him, it should've been me. And did the two of you get in a fight?"

"Who? Me and Krush?"

"What does Krush have to do with this?"

"Well...uh...he helped me out. You know, sobered me up, got me together."

"You were drunk?" she exclaimed, horrified.

"Isn't that what we're talking about?"

"No," she said sharply. "We're talking about you telling Touch about us."

"Huh?"

"He turned up at my apartment a few minutes ago, and he looks awful. You did get in a fight, didn't you?" she said accusingly.

"Are you kidding me? We did not get into a fight, and I sure as hell didn't tell him about us."

"Then how does he know?" They both said it at the same time.

"Krush!"

"That son-of-a-bitch," Famous exclaimed.

"How could he?" Shemika wailed.

"I'm coming over," Famous said, making a quick decision. "We gotta face this together."

"No!" she said helplessly. "If you come over, it'll only make things worse."

"There's no way you're handling it alone. I'll be there as soon as I can. Hang in there, Shemika. I promise you; everything's gonna be okay."

She put down the phone as Touch emerged from the bathroom. Yes, he did look beat up, there were gaping rips in his pants legs, and one of his exposed knees was dripping blood.

"I, I don't know what to say, Touch," she began. "I never meant for you to find out like this."

"Listen to me carefully, Shemika," he said urgently, ignoring her words. "If anyone asks, I was here all night."

"Excuse me?" she said, frowning.

"All night," he repeated. "You understand?"

She was utterly confused. Did he know about her and Famous or not? And if he did, it was obvious he had something else on his mind.

"I'm sorry to use you as my alibi," he continued, "but I witnessed something tonight. If the police think I was there, I'll get dragged into it, and that won't be good."

"Witnessed what?"

"Something bad."

"How bad?"

"It's better you don't know."

Suddenly she felt sick. Her mother's words came drifting back into her head. "Touch is not a victim, Shemika. His wife has been brutally murdered, and the suspicion lies on him."

"What's going on, Touch?" she asked, pulling her robe tightly around her.

"I told you," he said, sitting on the edge of the bed. "it's better you don't know."

"If you want me to say you were here, I have to know what I'm shielding you from."

"Jesus Christ!" he said furiously, standing up again. "Why can't you do as I say for once?"

She'd never seen this side of him before, this angry person she barely recognized.

"Does, does this have something to do with Sadiya's murder?" she asked tentatively.

"Fuck!" he exclaimed, walking over and banging his fist against the wall. "Fuck! Fuck! FUCK!"

"I don't understand what's going on," she said, moving across the room to get away from him. "But whatever it is, I think you'd better go."

"I come to you for help, and you're sending me away?" he said incredulously. "This is goddamn serious, Shemika. You'd better do as I tell you." He began to move towards her. She backed away.

"What's the matter with you?" he demanded. "I ask you to do one simple thing, and you can't. I'm your future husband. We're getting married."

His words filled her with dread. She'd thought she was in love with Touch, but it dawned on her that she had never been. He'd represented safety, and now he didn't. Finally, she realized that she would never have slept with another man if she'd really been in love with him. Too much to drink or not, it simply wasn't possible.

All she wanted at this moment was to get him out of her apartment.

"Are you just going to stand there and say nothing?" he yelled. "Jesus Christ, Shemika. I thought I could depend on you."

"If you tell me what's going on, then maybe I can help," she said, her voice sounding higher than usual. "However, if you don't..." Her words trailed off as she remembered that Famous was on his way over, and if Touch didn't know about them, the timing of his finding out couldn't have been worse.

"Forget it," Touch snapped. "I'm out of here. You're not the girl that I thought you were, Shemika. You're not someone I can trust." With that, he stormed his way to the front door.

She stayed in her bedroom, rooted to the spot, allowing him to go. Something very bad had happened for Touch to be acting like this. Something very, very bad.

And then the thought popped into her head, was Touch responsible for Sadiya's murder? Had he killed her? Shuddering with a sudden icy fear, she ran into the hall and locked the front door behind him.

***

Muttering to himself, Touch made it downstairs. He was furious with Shemika. This was the first time he'd ever asked her for anything, and it floored him that she couldn't manage to come through.

The problem was she was too young to understand what was going on. She wasn't a woman; she was a girl. A very lovely and innocent girl, but maybe thinking they could make a marriage work was a mistake. She wasn't that great with Camryn, and Camryn needed a mother, now more than ever.

The image of Irena sitting in her chair with a bullet hole through her forehead flashed through his mind. Who had killed her? And why?

Christ! What was happening? Why did everything seem to be spiraling out of control? He had to get a grip, decide what to do.

Stepping out of the elevator, he came face to face with Famous. "What the hell are you doing here?" he said, frowning.

"Okay, okay," Famous began, speaking fast. "I need to explain that it wasn't anyone's fault. It was one of those crazy things that just kinda happened. We didn't plan it. I can promise you that. I had no idea who she was, and she certainly had no clue I was your brother. It was kinda...fate."

Touch stared at his younger half-brother, the "fuck-up" as Red always referred to him. Was he missing something? Earlier, when he'd hammered on Shemika's door, she'd thought it was Famous. Now, why would she think Famous was at her door in the middle of the night?

It didn't make sense...or did it?

And then her words came back to him, "I, I don't know what to say...it wasn't planned...It just happened."

Almost the same words as Famous had used. And Shemika wasn't herself. She was nervous and jumpy, almost guilty.

Of what?

"Tell me about the crazy thing that just happened?" Touch demanded, a wave of helpless anger coursing through him, for he knew he was not going to like what he heard.

"You can't take it out on Shemika," Famous said earnestly. "You gotta understand that it wasn't her fault. She'd had too much to drink and, like I said, it was just one of those crazy things—"

Touch got it. Without thinking, he hauled back and slammed his fist into Famous's chin. Hard. "You son-of-a-bitch!" he screamed. "You fucking son-of-a-bitch!"

Famous swayed on his feet. "I'm telling you–you gotta understand," he yelled. "I love her, and she feels the same way about me. There's nothing you can do."

"Nothing, huh?" Touch screamed, all the anger and frustration of the past few days reaching boiling point. "You fucking asshole loser."

"You're just like Red," Famous managed, rubbing his chin. "Same lousy attitude. Same freaking words."

"Don't ever compare me to him."

"Jeez, Touch, I feel sorry for you because you are like him. Why don't you admit it? You're two of a kind."

Touch experienced a cold knot of fear and anger in the pit of his stomach. He was losing everything, including his fucking mind. However, he was not about to lose his identity. He would never be the man his father was. Never.

Without saying another word, he hurried from the building, got into his car, and drove home.

After a few tense minutes of deliberation and a stiff drink, he called his lawyer, then Krush, and finally Detective Banks.

The truth was, he had nothing left to lose.

Von Diesel

Chapter Fifteen

Early on Thursday morning, Velvet and Tristin sat together at the caterer's table on the beach eating breakfast. It was the last day of her photoshoot, and even though it had only been three days, she already knew how much she was going to miss everyone. Being fussed over was quite addictive and having Tristin in L.A. was the cream in her coffee. Not only was he capable of giving her a future career, but she found him to be incredibly sexy, interesting, and generous.

She'd never felt this way about a man before. Just being with him was a total trip, and it had nothing to do with the way everyone treated him like a star with all the trimmings, the limos, clubs, and expensive restaurants. To her, he was Tristin. Just a guy. And she'd fallen big-time.

"Last night, I was thinking about Cabo, and, yeah, I was about to say yes," she said, sipping a glass of freshly squeezed orange juice.

"Keep talking."

"Then my mom called, and here's the real reason I can't go."

"Spill."

"She needs to tell me something, and according to her, it's about my dad, and it's important."

"How important?"

"I don't know until I get back to New York."

"And two days is gonna make a difference?" he said, leaning in and giving her one of his intense looks.

She was silent for a moment. Then she said, "You can't understand. It's too personal."

"Try me."

"You see, I only have my mom, never had a dad, and it was only a few days ago she told me who he was. Now she's ready to change her story, so that's why I have to get back. I need to find out who I am."

"You're you," Tristin said quietly. "You always gotta remember that."

"I knew you wouldn't understand."

"You're wrong, baby," he said, looking into her eyes. "I understand bigtime."

"You're always—"

"Quit giving me that always shit like I don't get it," he interrupted, narrowing his eyes. "You wanna hear 'bout me? I'll tell you. My grandma raised me and my brother in the projects. We didn't have anything except her love and encouragement. That woman worked two jobs to keep us going. She was never too busy to teach me that if I wanted something, really wanted it, then I'd better shift my lazy ass and make it happen. And that's exactly what I did."

"I didn't know that," Velvet said.

"No reason you should. That's private shit I keep to myself. Nobody's business except mine."

"Where's your grandma now?"

"Living in a fancy house, I bought her in Brooklyn with my brother, his wife, and their three kids," he said. "I give that lady anything she damn well wants. She worked her ass off for me and my little bro, and she deserves the world."

"How about your parents? Are they around?"

"Never met either of them. I don't even know if they're still alive. Don't even give a crap."

"Why?" she asked curiously.

"Mom was a crackhead, my old man a dealer," he said flatly. "A coupla drugged-out freaks. They left us on our own 'til Grandma came and took us in. If it wasn't for her, we would've been pushed into the foster system."

"I'm sorry," she said softly. "It must have been tough for you."

"Hey," he said, shrugging, "you go with the breaks. My belief is you give props to the person who raised you, can't be worrying 'bout no one else. My grandma is the best woman in the world."

Before she could say anything, Quinn came over to inform her it was time to get to the make-up trailer. Reluctantly she got up to leave.

"So, don't go backing away from Cabo," Tristin said, standing up. "It's something we'll both get off on. You can figure out your family shit when we get back."

"You think?"

"I know, baby. I know."

"Sure, you do," she said, smiling at his supreme confidence. "You seem to know everything."

"Ain't that the truth," he said, grinning.

"Mr. Big Ego," she murmured.

"And don't you forget it."

"I'll try not to," she teased.

"See ya later, LL," he said and began strolling off down the beach.

"Shame he's straight," Quinn murmured. "Such a diabolical waste!"

"I'm sure his wife doesn't think so," she said tartly. "He's married, you know."

"My! My!" Quinn deadpanned. "I'd never have guessed."

She watched Tristin as he headed towards the hotel. He was everything she'd ever wanted in a man…and yet he was a married man, and she'd never been into sharing.

"Come along, dear," Quinn said crisply. "Time to stop lusting and come beautify."

"I'm not lusting," she objected, although she knew perfectly well that she was.

"You could've fooled me."

Sitting in the make-up chair, she still couldn't stop thinking about him. Now that he'd revealed a small part of his personal story, she was anxious to hear more. Tristin was an inspiration; he'd made it from nothing and look at him now. He was only thirty-six, a man who'd put himself out there and made a huge success doing something he loved. He wasn't just some rich hip-hop mogul with his own record label, he'd worked hard to get where he was, and it must have been quite a jump from nothing to everything.

The great American dream. Tristin was it.

It occurred to her that getting back to New York didn't seem so urgent. Whatever her mom had to say could wait. After all, she'd waited nineteen years to hear the truth. What difference would one weekend make?

Besides, Tristin was right. If she was going to achieve anything, it was because of her efforts. It didn't matter who her father was; he was long gone. She was her own person. It was time to stop feeling sorry for herself and seize everything life had to offer. Right now, there was a trip to Cabo staring her in the face, and if Tristin's wife didn't care, why should she?

For the morning shoot, she was wearing a slinky, soft black-leather Versace gown, so glamorous she was almost scared to move. It was slashed in the front all the way to the top of her thigh while the back dipped dangerously low. Teddy piled her hair on top of her head, and Uma had procured a million dollars' worth of Bentley and emerald jewelry from Neil Lane, the king of the estate jewelry business. Neil himself came to the shoot and couldn't stop raving about how fantastic his jewels looked on her.

When she finally hit the beach, she was barefoot and flawless.

"Phew!" Chip was blown away when he saw her. "This'll be the cover shot. No doubt in my mind."

"Not one of the swimsuit shots?" she asked. "Isn't showing flesh what this new magazine is all about?"

"Believe me. This shot's gonna beat them all," Chip assured her. "You got that Halle Berry mixed with Angelina Jolie thing going. Only younger and sexier. You're amazing!"

Amazing! Yes! Everything was amazing. A week ago, she'd been toiling away as a waitress, and now here she was in L.A., wearing Versace and posing for the cover of a magazine. It was all too much! An adventure she'd never believed possible.

Tristin came back in time for an early lunch break.

Before she was able to give him a positive response about Cabo, the caterer appeared with a huge cake, chocolate decorated with strawberries, the image of her face re-created in the center.

"What's this?" she exclaimed in surprise. "It's not my birthday."

"No, it's a big thank-you from all of us," Chip said, a crooked grin going full force as he mingled with all the people involved in the photoshoot. "We wanted your first modeling experience to be memorable. Everyone, gather round. We're taking a photo for posterity."

Tristin started to move away while Chip began to set up the shot with one of his assistants.

"Tristin," she said, calling him back boldly. "I want you in it too."

"This is your deal, LL," he said, uncharacteristically low-key. "Go ahead and shine. I'm not a part of it."

"Yes, you are," she insisted. "A very special part."

"Don't tell me my charm's finally melting that stony heart of yours?" he said, a slight smile hovering on his lips.

"Shut up and get over here," she said, grinning. "I want you in this picture."

"Yes, ma'am," he said, mock-saluting.

"Oh, and by the way," she added.

"What you got for me now?"

"I'm on for Cabo."

"Yeah?"

"Separate rooms."

"The lady builds me up just so she can let me down," he said wryly. "She gives with one hand, takes away with the other."

"That's the deal. Are we going?"

"Damn straight, we're going. Gotta hunch you and I are gonna make sweet, sweet soul music."

Chapter Sixteen

On Thursday morning, Fatima got out of bed at the usual time, but instead of dressing quickly and heading straight to the kitchen in the main house, she took time and applied her make-up carefully, then styled her hair. After that was done, she chose a simple but stylish blue dress, then added a couple of pieces of gold jewelry left over from her days as a singer. If Red insisted that she be at his meeting, she certainly wasn't about to walk in looking like the dowdy housekeeper.

She stood back and appraised her appearance in the mirror. The transformation was quite startling. Like her daughter, Fatima was a beauty, a darker beauty than Velvet, but stunning with her green eyes, full lips, and clouds of jet-black hair.

It was strange seeing herself all done up. It had been so long since she'd got herself together. Why now?

She knew why.

Something big was about to take place. Something that would startle everyone. Although perhaps not Lady Bentley, for she'd obviously, somehow or other, found out her and Red's secret. However, Red's three sons would be shocked, and so would Velvet, if only she was here. Fatima had begged her to hurry back to New York, but, as usual, Velvet was stubborn. She did things her way.

Fatima thought about her daughter for a moment. When she'd been forced to send Velvet away to live with Aretha, she'd lost all control over her. Always a wild child, Velvet had grown up fast and furious. Fatima often thanked God for Malshonda, at least Velvet wasn't out on her own. She had her cousin to protect her.

Von Diesel

Fatima sighed. There'd been no one to protect her when she'd left home at sixteen and arrived in New York. No one at all.

***

Fatima Dozier got off the bus from Atlanta, full of excitement and big dreams. She was in New York. New York City! And even though she had only a small amount of money, her desire to succeed as perhaps the new Anita Baker or Diana Ross outweighed all the disadvantages she might face. She could sing, she was good-looking, she'd imagined it was all going to be so damn easy.

But no. Nothing was easy for a pretty black girl alone and broke in New York.

For two years, she persevered, scoring a few gigs here and there. Along the way, she'd hooked up with a series of jazz musicians, not a good idea, for they all treated her in a cavalier way, passing her from one to the other.

One day, at a recording session, she ran into Zippy Ventura, a two-bit manager who talked a big game and liked what he saw. "You do for me, kiddo, and I'll do for you," he told her.

Zippy was a short, skinny white man in his forties. He was married to Kandie, a tough-looking black woman with bleached, white-blonde hair and enormous fake breasts.

Marriage didn't seem to hinder Zippy, who was after any outside-his marriage action he could get. In exchange for the occasional grope in his seedy office, he began to score Fatima quite a few decent gigs singing background at sessions and, even better, solo spots at a late-night club, Gloria's in Harlem.

Gloria, a large gay woman, took an immediate shine to Fatima, nicknaming her Dini and constantly lecturing her on the joys of being with a woman as opposed to a man.

Fatima was not convinced, although she could certainly have done without Zippy and his lascivious moves.

Fatima sang at the club twice a week. Standing on the small smoky stage, belting out jazz versions of standards like "You Go To My Head" and "But Not For Me", she felt very much like she was heading for the big-time.

Men chased her, especially the regular customers, but after her bad experiences with musicians, she'd kind of given up on men.

One night, Red Bentley showed up. Fatima had no idea who he was, but a very impressed Zippy and Gloria soon filled her in: Red Bentley was a much-married billionaire media tycoon with a fierce reputation. Zippy and Gloria were over the moon that he'd chosen to spend time at Gloria's.

After his first visit, Red Bentley returned several times, sometimes with a woman, sometimes alone. He sat at a front table and never took his eyes off her as she went through her repertoire of old standards.

"He likes you," Zippy informed her.

"So what?" was her reply.

"He wants you to have a drink with him," Gloria informed her.

"Not me," was her reply.

This went on for several weeks until one night Zippy cornered her and said, "You're gonna sit down and have a drink with him, or you're outta a job."

Red Bentley was sixty. Fatima was eighteen. This didn't seem to bother either Zippy or Gloria, so she sat down and had a drink with him.

Red insisted she drink champagne, even though she was underage.

She obliged.

He plied her with compliments, telling her he thought she was beautiful and sexy and ripe.

Ripe? she thought. What does he mean by ripe?

"I want to fuck you," he said.

"No way," she said.

A week later, Zippy told her that if she didn't sleep with Red Bentley, she was out of a job.

Nice. But she had nothing to lose except her job, so she did it.

The experience wasn't bad, and it wasn't good. It was just...nothing. Fatima was ashamed of herself for sleeping with a rich old man just to keep working. It wasn't right, and she knew it. However, she reconciled herself to it: he wasn't the first man she'd slept with, and he certainly wouldn't be the last.

After that night, Red Bentley stopped coming to the club.

"What didja do to turn him off?" Zippy demanded, left eye twitching as he stared at her accusingly.

"Nothing," she answered blankly.

"You happy now?" Gloria complained to Zippy. "You made her sleep with him, and now we lost us a big-time customer."

Fatima couldn't care less. All she wanted to do was sing. It didn't bother her that Red never came back.

Six weeks later, she realized she was pregnant. She kept the news to herself until it was too late to have an abortion, whereupon she informed Zippy and Gloria that she had to go home to Atlanta and visit her family for a while. Then she took a job as a receptionist in a beauty salon on Lexington, working up until three weeks before her baby was born.

Fatima named her baby Velvet for freedom. And when Velvet was six weeks old, she contacted Zippy. She told him she was back in the city and needed work.

He grumbled that she'd been away too long. The small following she'd started to acquire had moved on.

"Don't you want to be my manager?" she asked him.

"You do for me, and—"

"No!" she said, backing away from his hands-on approach. "It's business or nothing."

"Go find yourself a new manager," he muttered, quite insulted that she would turn him down.

So, she did. She found Fred Marks, an energetic go-getter who immediately booked her into a series of clubs, some as far away as Atlantic City. It didn't matter. At least she was making enough money to pay her rent and hire a woman to take care of Velvet when she was working.

Fatima adored her baby. She thought Velvet was the most beautiful little creature she'd ever seen. Sometimes, when people found out she had a child, they wanted to know who Velvet's daddy was. Fatima came up with a variety of stories, none of them true. She had no desire for Red Bentley to find out that he'd fathered her child. She could manage very nicely without him. Although sometimes, when things were slow, it was quite a struggle.

Right after Velvet's fifth birthday, she met a man she liked. His name was Leon, and they were both singing back-up for some female one-hit-wonder. They bonded over coffee and complaints about how bad the singer was. Two weeks later, Leon moved in with her, which was a big help because he immediately took over half of the expenses. The other good news was that he fell in love with Velvet, and she with him. The two were sweet together, and Fatima knew that if

Leon asked her to marry him, she would do so without a moment's hesitation.

But Leon didn't ask, and one year together turned into two. Fatima realized she wasn't getting any younger, and no big breaks were staring either of them in the face, so she broke up with him.

Velvet was devastated. To her, Leon was Mr. Daddy, and for him to abandon her was extremely painful. She was only seven, but it was the start of the trouble between her and Fatima.

Fred did his best, but as time passed, the gigs became fewer and fewer, girl jazz singers were out of style. So, one night Fatima decided to revisit Gloria's.

The club was still open, and there, mingling with her customers was Gloria herself, big and warm and welcoming. Unfortunately, Zippy was still around, too, pushing a young singer he insisted was the new Whitney Houston. Divorced and bitter, he was not pleased to see Fatima, but Gloria was. She invited her back to sing at the club three nights a week.

Fatima gladly accepted, which pissed Zippy off, causing an angry rift between him and Gloria. This was a relief to Fatima because now she didn't have to deal with Zippy and his wandering hands.

"Zippy's got himself a little problem," Gloria confided, pantomiming someone sniffing a line of coke.

It wasn't long before Gloria found out about Velvet, who was now nine and quite a budding beauty.

"When did she happen?" Gloria exclaimed.

Fatima made up an old boyfriend back in Atlanta. Gloria seemed to accept her story, and as a special treat, Fatima sometimes brought Velvet to the club to listen to her sing.

One night Zippy turned up. He was an unexpected and unwelcome visitor.

The Billionaire Bentleys

Unfortunately, it was a night when Velvet was there, standing at the side of the stage watching her mother perform.

Zippy slobbered all over the child while Fatima was singing, telling her how pretty she was and how he was her mom's best friend, so they should all get together more often.

"Where's your daddy?" he asked.

"Don't have a daddy," Velvet replied, thinking what a funny-looking man Zippy was.

"How old are you?"

"Nine."

"Nine, huh? When you gonna be ten?"

"May the first," she said proudly.

"I'll buy you a present," Zippy promised, his almost coke-addled brain figuring out a thing or two.

When Fatima got offstage, she was furious. She and Zippy became involved in a loud argument, which finished when Gloria intervened and threw him out.

Fatima had a hunch that she had not seen the last of Zippy, and she was right. A week later, he turned up at her apartment. "I know whose kid she is," he said, taunting her. "The dates fit, so don't go thinking you can fool me." She blanked him.

He was insistent.

"Does Red have any idea he has a kid with you?" Zippy asked, trying to force his way past her into her apartment.

She was sure he must be bluffing. How could he possibly know? And why would he even care?

She told him that he was crazy, that he should go away and leave her alone, or she'd call the police.

Zippy laughed in her face. "Ya dumb bitch. Don't you know this means big fucking bucks? We gotta partner up and take the old guy for a bundle." Fatima called the police to get him to stop bothering her.

She was a black woman, and Zippy was a white man. The police did nothing.

A few days later, Zippy accosted Velvet outside her school. He reminded her that he was a good friend of her mom's and that he had the present he'd promised her. He took her to a nearby coffee shop.

Velvet went with him willingly. Since she'd met him at the club, she figured he was her mom's friend. Besides, he had a present for her.

Zippy ordered her a strawberry smoothie, then presented her with a cheap plastic manicure set. He extracted the nail clippers from the manicure set. "Gimme your hand," he said, "and Uncle Zippy will show you how to use it."

She did as he asked, and he clipped a couple of her nails. Then, as if by accident, he jammed the sharp part of the clippers into her wrist, drawing blood.

"Ouch!" she squealed.

Quick as a flash, he produced a cotton swab, soaked up the blood, and popped the swab into a small plastic bag.

"You hurt me," she complained. "I'm going home."

"Wait a minute," he said. "You got something caught in your hair." And he pulled out a couple of hairs.

"Ouch!" she squealed again.

"Don't worry 'bout it," he said, adding the hairs to his plastic bag. "You want another smoothie?"

When Velvet got home and told her mom where she'd been, Fatima went berserk. She accepted most things, but not a roach like Zippy messing with her daughter. How dare he?

She had no way of contacting him, but she was certain he'd come back, and when he did, she made sure she was ready. She purchased a handgun and learned how to use it. The next time Zippy came sniffing around, she planned on sticking it in his stomach and telling him that if he ever went near her daughter again, she'd blow his brains out.

Two weeks later, he turned up at her apartment on a Saturday night. He was not alone. He was accompanied by Red Bentley. The two men marched into her small apartment as if they owned it. She was too startled to stop them. Fortunately, Velvet was away, spending the weekend with a school friend.

"Where's the kid?" Zippy demanded as if he had a right to know.

Red Bentley glared at her with cold, hard eyes. "You had the nerve to give birth to my child," he thundered. "How dare you? Who do you think you are?"

He had aged since she'd last seen him. He seemed smaller and more wrinkled. It crossed her mind that she should never have slept with him. But if she hadn't done so, she wouldn't have Velvet, and Velvet made every day worthwhile.

"What do you want?" she said flatly.

"No. The point is, what do you want?" Red asked coldly. "What blackmailing scheme have you and your cohort come up with?"

She didn't know what cohort meant, but she did understand that he was referring to Zippy. He was standing there with a big shit-eating grin on his stupid face as if he'd just discovered America.

"A million bucks should do it," Zippy said, winking at her as if they were co-conspirators. "A million bucks, and then we'll go away, and you'll never hear from us again."

"Is that all?" Red drawled sarcastically. "Surely you should demand more than that?"

"Huh?" Zippy blurted, left eye twitching out of control. "You want the kid? She's a pretty little thing. For another two mill, you can have her."

Fatima stared at Zippy in horror. Who did he think he was? He had no rights over her child. This was insane.

"My lawyers can make you very sorry you ever thought up this scheme to get money out of me," Red said, fairly calmly. "I came here tonight to see if I remembered the black bitch I slept with. Yes, I do remember her. She was no good then, and she's no good now." A long pause. "Tell me, did you two morons honestly believe you could get away with blackmailing Red Bentley? You can't be that stupid?"

Suddenly, Fatima found her voice. "Get out of my apartment," she said in a low, angry voice. "Both of you. Right now!"

Zippy threw her a furious look. He'd thought when she heard the amount of money involved that she'd acquiesce and shut the fuck up. But, no, she was too dumb to do that.

"Oh," Red said. "So now you're going to play good cop, bad cop. A little late in the day for that game, don't you think?"

Fatima turned to him. "I'm not after your money. I want nothing from you." She indicated Zippy. "This piece of garbage here is speaking on my behalf, and he has no right. He has nothing to do with me. Nothing." Tears filled her eyes at the injustice of it all.

"Excuse me, chickie," Zippy said quickly, trying to save a situation that could turn on him. "I discovered you. You owe everything to me. So, stop acting like an ungrateful bitch, and accept the money Mr. Bentley's gonna give us for keeping our mouths shut tight 'bout his little black bastard."

Fatima began to lose it. "Our mouths?" she shouted. "Velvet's mine, and she's not for sale. Both of you, get out now."

Zippy moved toward her. "Wimmin!" he said, rolling his eyes at Red. "They're always changing their damn minds. We had an agreement, you know." He grabbed her wrist in a steel-like grip. "Shut up," he muttered so that only she could hear him. "You're gonna blow this sweet deal if you don't shut yer fucking mouth."

Fatima was in shock. How could this be happening? What had she done to deserve such treatment?

"A million bucks," Zippy whispered. "He'll pay, and we'll split it right down the middle, and you get to keep ya kid."

Something came over her, a rage so deep that she was rendered almost speechless. Zippy was the lowest of the low, and he was trying to make her his partner. He was dragging Red Bentley into her life, upsetting everything.

"Get out," she hissed.

"I ain't going nowhere, honey, not until you see your way to agree to this. And if ya don't, I'll make sure your little girl's life ain't gonna be worth living."

Very calmly, she snatched her wrist out of Zippy's grasp. She walked over to the shelf where she kept her handgun hidden behind a pile of magazines.

"I think we got us a deal at one million big ones," Zippy said confidently, turning to Red.

"You are a very ignorant man," Red began to say, "and I do not do business with—"

Before Red could finish his sentence, Fatima pulled out her gun and, hands shaking, pointed it at Zippy. "Get...out," she repeated.

He blanched visibly at the sight of her pointing a gun at him. "Now hold on a minute, ch-chickie," he stammered. "Ya gotta put that thing down."

"What kind of a scam do the two of you think you're pulling?" Red roared, stepping between them. "I'm not some out-of-town mark who'll fall for this phony show you're putting on."

"The broad's crazy," Zippy said, left eye twitching out of control as he sensed the money slipping away. "A crazy bitch with your kid. You should take the damn kid away from her. She ain't nothing but a two-bit slut, and if the kid stays with her, she'll turn out the same freaking way. Give us two mil for the girl, and you'll be getting yourself a real fine bargain. I can personally—"

With all the strength she could muster, Fatima shoved Red aside and went for Zippy, forgetting she held the gun.

Red moved in to stop the fight. The three of them struggled, locked together for a few moments, and then bang. The gun went off, and Zippy slid to the ground.

***

Fatima took one final look in the mirror. She was still attractive, she thought, still able to command the attention of men if she so desired.

She did not so desire.

She was thirty-eight years old, and she'd shut herself off from the world for nine long years. Nine years of looking after Red Bentley, seeing he had everything he needed, never straying far from the house on 68th Street.

It was safer that way.

Now Red Bentley was prepared to reveal a part of their secret, but not the secret about Zippy. Oh no, that was something nobody would ever find out, something only they shared.

Fatima held her head high and made her way upstairs. Whatever happened next, she was determined to face it with dignity.

Chapter Seventeen

At first, they'd fought, and then they'd made up. Making up was so delightful that when Shemika stirred to the sound of her phone ringing, she was in a lighthearted, happy mood. It was Thursday morning, and the sun was shining. Touch knew the truth about her and Famous, so no more guilt.

Well…a little bit of guilt because last night had not been pretty. Touch had shown a side of himself that she'd never seen before, a frightening side.

Famous lay beside her, still asleep, snoring lightly. She picked up the phone, a smile on her lips, and was hit with a tirade from her usually controlled mother.

"Have you seen the filthy rags?" Nancy seethed. "Do you know what they're saying? Our family name is being dragged through the mud. This is a disgrace! I will sue every one of these disgusting so-called journalists."

"Calm down, Mother."

"No! You calm down."

"I'm not the one yelling."

"You will be when you read this garbage," Nancy said ominously.

"Why are you reading it anyway?"

"How can I not, when the staff is all gathered in the kitchen laughing at us."

"I'm sure they aren't."

"Our connection with the Bentley family is finished. Finished," Nancy repeated sternly. "Do you understand me, Shemika?"

"Yes, Mother," Shemika said patiently. "I'll call you later."

She put the phone down and took another look at Famous. He was still sleeping. One arm was thrown casually across his eyes, stomach exposed, rippling abs and a very fine spattering of body hair. This was love, the feeling she had when she watched him sleep.

She wondered what the tabloids had written that had her mother so riled up. Nobody believed what they printed anyway, so why did it matter?

Last night, after she and Famous had made love, they'd lain in bed and talked for hours until they'd fallen asleep in each other's arms. This morning she felt as if a huge weight had been lifted from her. It was the biggest relief in the world to know she was free.

The more she thought about it, the more she realized just how wrong she and Touch had been together. Surely, he would realize it too. They simply hadn't fit. Movies. Music. Books. Their tastes were polar opposites. With Famous, everything was in sync. They both enjoyed adventure movies, listening to Coldplay and the Black Eyed Peas, and when it came to books, there was nothing like a good old John Grisham or James Siegel thriller. Even their TV preferences matched: *Alias* and *Seinfeld*. Famous had told her that in Milan, he'd caught the first two seasons of both shows on DVD.

How great was that? A man she could watch TV with. Touch had considered TV a total waste of time.

Momentous decision. Should she fix Famous breakfast? What would he like? Tea? Coffee? Did he take sugar and cream? Cereal or eggs?

She knew so little about him, yet she felt she knew everything. He'd told her about his drinking and drug days, the lost years wandering around New York like a zombie, sleeping with anyone and everyone, shit-faced and out of his mind most of the time.

He'd got into a few family horror stories. His abusive father. His alcoholic mother. The beatings he'd received and his fractured childhood being shuttled back and forth between the two of them.

Then Italy and his recovery. And Kareema, whom he swore he didn't love. "I love you, Shemika," he'd said. "You're it for me. I'm through with other women. Over. Done."

"Really?" she'd asked, tilting her head on one side.

"Yeah, really," he'd replied, a huge grin on his face.

She smiled as she thought about his words. I'm through with other women. Over. Done.

How high school. How very sweet. How much she loved him.

***

Krush awoke to a cup of strong black coffee and a nagging ache in his gut. He hadn't had much sleep, a couple of hours at most. In the early hours of the morning, he'd received an urgent call from Touch, so he'd hauled himself out of bed and hurried over to his brother's apartment, where he'd found Elliott Minor and Detective Banks.

It seemed that Touch had been at a murder scene and had not immediately reported it to the police. And there was also the matter of Sadiya's box. Evidence that Touch had taken from her apartment and kept to himself, only handing it over now.

Some mess, but Elliott was definitely a lawyer with well-placed connections, and after a few phone calls to the right people, Touch was exonerated of any guilt and left with a stern warning about not withholding any more crucial information concerning Sadiya.

"You got off easy," Krush told him after everyone had taken off. But before he could make a quick exit, Touch had launched into a long diatribe about Shemika and Famous. Somehow or other, he'd found out about them, which meant that Krush had been obliged to spend the next two hours smoothing out Touch's bruised feelings and persuading him not to have Famous beaten up and tossed in the East River.

What a night! No rest for the weary. And in between, he fielded calls from Chilly Rose, Lola Sanchez, Gregory Dark, and Damiun Likely, four of his most important clients. Chilly was carrying on about her upcoming wedding, Lola wanted to sue a chasing paparazzo who'd slammed into the back of her new Ferrari on purpose, Gregory was demanding more of the backend from his upcoming studio deal, and Damiun was claiming he'd met a girl, fallen in love, and would marry her within days.

Nuts. They were all totally nuts.

Now he had the meeting with Red to look forward to. It should be a laugh a minute with both his brothers there. He couldn't wait.

In the meantime, he was desperate to get back to the comparative sanity of L.A. He was even considering not breaking up with Chandra, his current girlfriend in L.A. Chandra could, when she wanted, be quite a calming influence, which was exactly what he needed right now, a little peace and calm. Besides, his house would need redecorating, so who better than Chandra to take care of it?

The downside was that she would expect to move in. *Why not?* he thought. But only for a few months while she gets everything organized.

He could handle it. After the past week, he could handle just about anything.

***

Elliott Minor was worth every penny of his quite exorbitant fees. Having come clean on everything to Detective Banks, Touch had expected to spend at least a few hours down at the precinct answering questions, but Elliott had made sure that didn't happen, although Touch could tell that the detective was royally pissed after receiving a call from his captain.

By that time, Touch hadn't given a shit. He'd had a tough night, and all he wanted was to swallow a couple of Ambien and sleep it off.

In the morning, he lay in bed, experiencing an overall bad feeling. His first thoughts were of Shemika, his once perfect Shemika. It was over. She'd betrayed him. He'd never expected it of her. For not only had she betrayed him, but she'd also done so with his own brother. This left a sour taste in his mouth. Famous he could understand. But Shemika? Oh, no, not Shemika, his innocent bride-to-be.

Bride-to-be no more. He was finished with her. She'd slept with his brother. There was no going back.

He reached for the phone, called Mrs. Conner, and checked on Camryn. Mrs. Conner informed him that everything was fine and that Camryn was having a lovely time.

Just thinking about his little girl made him break out in a sweat. What if she wasn't his? What if Draygo or Alex or who the fuck else Sadiya had slept with was Camryn's real father?

Christ! He couldn't bear it. It simply wasn't possible.

And yet…it was.

So, what was he supposed to do? Arrange a DNA test?

No! He wasn't about to do that. Camryn was his. There was no doubt in his mind.

Or was there?

***

Because Red was so rich, people always got it into their stupid heads that he was the perfect person to extort. Surely, they understood that to become the man he was today. He had not suffered fools easily. He was a destroyer, and those who were foolish enough to get in his way were duly destroyed.

Yesterday, some low-down Russian hooker had made her move. It infuriated him when people made the mistake of treating him as if he was an easy mark. Especially women. Especially whores.

The truth, according to Red Bentley, was that, at some time or another, all women behaved like whores. They all had a price. It was a question of finding out how much. And he should know, he'd married four.

Four wives, and not a winner among them.

As for Lady J Bentley, she'd turned out to be the most expensive whore of all. And she couldn't even suck a cock properly, so what good was she?

He would pay her off and good riddance. But she would not get as much as she was asking for, no damn way.

He was Red Bentley. A self-made man to be reckoned with. Nobody ever got the better of him, although many had tried. In business, he was a killer. He conducted his personal life the same way. Only the strongest survived in Red Bentley's world.

He thought about the red-headed call-girl for a moment. Spectacular looking. Zaftig and Russian–the kind of woman he got off on. Spewing crap about Sadiya. What did he care? Sadiya was dead, and he wasn't the fool who'd married her. Touch was. His eldest son. His eldest idiot.

Why couldn't his sons have been more like him? They all took after their useless mothers, and that was a real shame.

None of them had the kind of balls he possessed. Brass balls. Solid brass.

Red looked forward to the meeting that lay ahead; it should be quite an event. His three sons, Lady J and Fatima. Some combination.

They were probably all stressing over why he'd called the meeting.

Well soon, they would find out.

It was time.

Von Diesel

Chapter Eighteen

Lady J Bentley was the first to arrive in the library. It was a magnificent room with its dark wood floor-to-ceiling bookcases, stiff leather couches, and rare Persian rugs.

She ran her fingers across the mantel, picking up a residue of dust. Damned maids, they did nothing. During her time with Red, he'd never allowed her to fire any of them, claiming that terminating staff was his privilege. He hired and fired on a whim, savoring every moment.

Now she knew why he'd kept that insolent housekeeper around. Fatima. Mother of his illegitimate child, a child she'd never even heard of until she'd discovered the revealing letter tucked into his safe.

It was a lawyer's letter, very clear and to the point. It stated that although Red Bentley had fathered Fatima's daughter, Fatima would never reveal this publicly or tell her daughter, Velvet, who her father was. Fatima also relinquished any claims on his estate, and in return, she would receive a one-time payment of five hundred and fifty thousand dollars, paid out after he died, plus a lifetime job in his employ with her own apartment in the basement of his house. The letter was signed by Fatima and two independent witnesses.

Now, why? Lady J thought, Why would anyone sign a letter like that? The woman had given birth to Red Bentley's baby. With a good lawyer, she could probably have had anything she wanted. It was inexplicable. Was Fatima that dense?

Probably. Dense and uneducated with no self-respect. Otherwise, she would never have signed such a letter. Anyway, it was about time the boys knew the truth, and today

Lady J decided she would take great pleasure in telling them that they had a sister.

Red would be livid. She didn't care. As soon as her attorney informed her that her settlement was agreed upon, she was out of there. Only why not cause a little trouble first? Since Red had invited her to attend this meeting, she may as well make the most of it.

Her attorney had warned her not to go. "The less you have to do with him, the stronger our position," he'd said. "You have nothing to gain."

But how could she resist seeing Red's crusty old face when she told his sons something she knew he never wanted them to find out?

She had dressed appropriately for the occasion. Hair swept up. Chanel suit. Gucci shoes. Two rows of perfect pearls. Discreet Bentley and pearl earrings. Cartier Bentley watch.

She'd spent the early part of the morning thumbing through some brochures of available properties. There was a Park Avenue penthouse that sounded perfect for entertaining. She'd made up her mind that, once she'd got out of this mausoleum, she was giving plenty of chic, exclusive dinner parties. Then again, there was a pre-war masterpiece on Sutton Place that reeked of elegant charm.

She had plenty of time to decide, and in the meantime, she'd take a suite at the St. Regis until she made up her mind. After all, she was destined to be a rich woman. Very rich indeed.

***

"Why are you going to a meeting with your father, a man who has never done anything for you?" Shemika had asked

Famous early in the morning. "Isn't it time you gave up hoping for any kind of relationship?"

He'd shrugged. She couldn't possibly understand. Nobody could. It was complicated.

"I'm going 'cause my brothers want me to," he'd replied, sitting at the breakfast counter, staring at Shemika, who was probably the prettiest girl he'd ever seen. And it wasn't just her physical attributes. There was something else about her, a sweetness, a sense of goodness. He was crazy in love, and this was a first.

"I doubt that Touch does," she'd said.

"This will be the last time I go there."

She nodded. He'd known she'd want to talk about it later. That was Shemika's way.

In the meantime, he'd showered, dressed, and set off for the meeting that should've taken place the previous week.

Why was he going? That was a good question. Touch probably wasn't speaking to him, and he couldn't blame his brother for that. Krush, a true Libra, would refuse to take sides.

Still…it was a family meeting, and Famous knew he was entitled to be there.

Later he'd made up his mind to call Draygo and ask her to set him up with a New York modeling agency. Even though he was a star in Italy, he didn't care to walk in anywhere cold. And since Draygo knew everyone, she could easily arrange an introduction and steer him to the best.

He considered this to be of the utmost importance. There was no way he was living off Shemika, so it was essential that he got his career off the ground in America. The Ciccone campaign was a brilliant start. Once the ads started appearing in all the American magazines, everything should fall into place.

And when he started making money, he was already thinking of asking Shemika to marry him.

Kind of a scary thought, but at the same time, he knew it was what he wanted—finally, a settled life.

***

After Famous had left her apartment, Shemika ran around cleaning up. She was singing, unable to wipe the smile off her face as she tackled her bed, shaking out the duvet and plumping up the pillows. Famous was it for her. Somehow or other, they just clicked. In bed. Out of bed. She was in love, no doubt about it.

Then she remembered her mother's phone call and figured she'd better take a look at the tabloids that had Nancy so upset. Best to get that little task dealt with before she went to work.

She slipped on jeans and a T-shirt, then ran downstairs to the newsvendor on the corner, where she picked up all the offending magazines.

Once home, she set them out on the kitchen counter and studied the coverage. Her mother was right. It was awful, scurrilous gossip of the worst kind. And the photos were horrendous, especially the ones of Famous stoned out of his head with various girls in major stages of undress.

She found it hard to understand why they were dragging Famous into this. He had had nothing to do with his brother's murdered wife. It simply wasn't fair.

Oh, God! Wait until Nancy found out that she'd switched brothers and was now with Famous. Oh, Lordy, there'd be raised voices in the Scott-Simon household.

Too bad. It was about time she stood up to her mother, and in the future, that was exactly what she intended to do.

***

The traffic was backed up, so Krush decided to walk to Red's house from the hotel. He'd thought about calling Famous on his cell, then reconsidered. *Do I really want to get in the middle of my two brothers?* he'd thought. *It's their fight. Let them work it out.*

On the way, he made a few calls. First, Lola Sanchez, his Latina diva whom he talked out of suing by explaining that going after a cheap-shot paparazzo was a big waste of time and money. Next, he called Gregory Dark and assured him he would do his best to secure him another couple of points on his studio deal. He didn't call Chilly Rose because it was too early in L.A. But he did call Damiun Likely, who was in Paris with his new girlfriend/fiancée, an eighteen-year-old actress.

"This is crazy," Krush informed him. "Too fast."

"I'm in love, man," Damiun enthused. "This girl is amazing!"

"Does this mean I need to get to work on the prenup?"

"I don't want to insult her."

Sure, Krush thought. *When she discovers you're gay, she won't be at all insulted.* "Hold off until she signs," he advised. "I'll have the papers to you first thing tomorrow."

Chandra was next on his list. She was cool and crisp as he explained why he hadn't called, blaming it on family problems, which was basically true. "How about meeting me at the airport? Then we'll stop by Koi's and grab a bite," he suggested, the old Krush Bentley charm going full force.

"I met a friend of yours," Chandra said, her tone quite icy.

"You did? Who was it?"

"Inez Fallon."

Oh, shit! Inez. The actress from the plane with whom he'd shared one night of energetic sex. "Ah, yes, Inez," he said, hoping Inez hadn't shot her mouth off. "Nice girl."

"She liked you too," Chandra said, her tone getting even colder. "Informed me you were a stud in bed, and she's expecting you to call her soon."

Busted! What kind of luck was that? "Look," he explained. "You and I, we were kind of on the outs, right?"

"Wrong." A long, meaningful beat. "So, Krush, here's what I suggest. Go fuck yourself." And Chandra clicked off, leaving him without a girlfriend.

Damn. He'd been quite looking forward to Chandra's professional backrubs and somewhat Zen blowjobs. Plus, he'd had her pegged to organize the redecorating of his house. Too bad.

Finally, standing outside Red's house, he called his assistant, Chi-rone, at home.

"Should I give you yesterday's phone list?" Chi-rone asked. "It's long."

"E-mail me. I'll go over it on the plane."

"A woman called Kareema phoned from Italy. She said she's coming to L.A. and wants to get together."

"Kareema, huh?" Krush said, flashing onto the extremely beautiful Kareema. Hmm…Things were looking up. He wasn't usually into sloppy seconds, but since Famous had definitely moved on… "Did she leave a number?" he asked.

"She did."

"E-mail it to me first."

"Right away."

"How's my house?"

"They've started work on it."

"Thanks, Chi-rone." He glanced up. Famous was approaching "Gotta go. See you later."

***

Isha was lurking in the underground parking garage of Touch's apartment building when he emerged from the basement elevator on his way to Red's house.

Earlier she'd observed all the press and camera crews outside the front, and she'd figured that when he left his apartment, it would be via the garage. So, she'd made her way down there, charming her way past the security guard with a smile. Isha had learned at a very early age that a seductive smile could get her anywhere she wanted.

She hung around somewhere between Touch's car and the elevator, waiting patiently. If Red Bentley didn't want to pay, she was sure Touch Bentley would. He had a child to protect. He would not relish the information she had about Sadiya being made public.

When he emerged, she was ready. "Mr. Bentley," she said, boldly approaching him.

"Who are you?" he said shortly. He'd just come off the phone with Elliott Minor, who'd informed him that Detective Banks had new evidence concerning Sadiya's murder and was close to making an arrest. This was surprising and startling news. Although not that startling, because once he'd told the detective about Draygo, he'd known something would happen.

"He'd like to contact you when an arrest takes place," Elliott said. "Where will you be?"

"I'm on my way to my father's house."

"We'll stay in touch," Elliott said.

"That's fine," Touch said.

Von Diesel

"I'm sorry about the tabloids," Elliott added. "We can sue the bastards if you give me the word."

Touch had no idea what Elliott was talking about. He hadn't seen the tabloids, and he didn't intend to.

"I am an acquaintance of your father's," Isha said. "He suggested you might have interest in certain…information."

Now, why would Red be sending this woman to see him? "About what?" Touch said, frowning.

"My wife?" he said, thinking how like Sadiya this woman sounded.

"About your wife. Your wife that is deceased."

"Who are you?"

"I am Isha. I know your brother also."

She looked vaguely familiar. Long, flaming-red hair, statuesque body. He'd seen her somewhere before. Then it came to him. The girl-on-girl show at his bachelor party. Jesus Christ! What the hell did she want?

"We must talk," Isha said.

"Not now," he said brusquely. "I'm on my way to a meeting."

"It is urgent," Isha said, licking her lips.

"It'll have to wait."

"Until when?"

Touch's patience was wearing thin. "Look, Miss," he said sharply, "what is it that you want?"

"Five hundred thousand dollars for my silence regarding Sadiya's marriage to a Russian man. They were never divorced. I have proof of their marriage. Money for silence. Is good American business, yes?"

First Draygo, and now this woman. Well, she was too late because he didn't care anymore. Soon Draygo would be arrested, and the world would know how he'd been duped by

194

Sadiya. So be it. He'd protect Camryn as best he could. That was all he could do.

He headed for his car. She followed close behind.

He stopped for a moment and swung his head round. "Did Draygo send you?"

She was startled that he knew Draygo's name.

"Well," Touch demanded, "did he?"

"You, you know about Draygo?"

"Get out of here before I report you to the police," he said sharply. "Blackmail is a Federal offense. You could go to jail. So, get the hell out of my way."

Isha was stunned. What was wrong with the Bentley family? They had plenty of money. Why didn't they pay?

Now it was her turn to frown. She would go to the newspapers; that was what she'd do. She would sell their dirty secrets for a lot more than five hundred thousand. And not only would she sell their secrets, but she'd embellish, add plenty of sex. After all, she'd fucked the father and the son. That should be worth plenty.

Red Bentley, billionaire sex pervert. Krush Bentley... Hmm, he'd not been into any freak scenes. She'd have to make something up.

Perhaps like father like son...

Yes, that was it. Who was there to refute her story?

Inka.

Ah, Inka. Perhaps it would be wise to bring Inka in on it. Not as a full partner. After all, it had not been Inka's idea; it was hers. However, with Inka involved, her story would have back-up, making it worth all the more.

Big bucks, Isha thought. That's what America is all about, big bucks.

***

Detective Banks had experienced a busy night. A high-profile murder always increased the pressure to get the case solved as fast as possible. As if it was easy. The way the jerks in the mayor's office were screaming for action was no big help.

Solving a murder case was like assembling an intricate jigsaw puzzle. You put it together, piece by piece until suddenly the picture is clear and everything else falls into place.

Touch Bentley producing Sadiya's box at one a.m. was a big help. Although, Detective Banks would have preferred to receive it at a more civilized hour and certainly earlier in his investigation. Over the last several days, he'd had very little sleep, so after hitting the sack at midnight, he had not appreciated being awoken at one a.m. on Thursday and summoned to Touch Bentley's apartment. Then there was the murder of Irena to consider. After listening to Touch's story, he'd dispatched a crime-squad team to Brighton Beach and got himself there somewhere around three a.m.

Now it was nine in the morning, and, after being up all night, he had Sadiya Bentley's killer in his sights.

Soon…very soon…he'd be the department's hero.

And why not? He'd worked damn hard on this one.

***

"Hey," Krush said.

"Hey," Famous responded as they exchanged an awkward hug. "Uh…thanks for last night," Famous continued. "Guess you kinda saved me from myself. Sorry I was such an asshole. Dunno what I was thinking. It was a big mistake. It won't happen again."

They were standing on the sidewalk outside Red's house, neither of them looking forward to going in.

"I don't see you carrying a bag," Krush remarked.

Famous pushed his hair out of his eyes. "A bag?"

"L.A.," Krush reminded him. "Remember? I booked you a ticket to come with me."

"Oh, yeah." A beat. "Uh…listen, Krush, thanks for the offer, but I can't go. You see, last night—"

"I know all about last night," Krush interrupted. "Touch called me. I went over to his place and heard the whole sorry story."

"Is he destroyed?"

"Do you want him to be?"

"No way. I got nothing against Touch. I wish I knew him better."

"That ain't gonna happen, little bro. Not when you tell him that he's exactly like Red."

"Oh, shit," Famous said, shaking his head. "I didn't mean to say that."

"Then why did you?"

"Because he punched me out, called me a loser," Famous explained. "I couldn't hit him back. I would've floored him. Guess I tried to hurt him with words."

"Right," Krush said. "So, you steal his fiancée, then tell him he's exactly like the father we all hate. Right on, little bro. That will really make him like you."

"Fuck!"

"Yeah, fuck. Let's go in."

Red watched from an upstairs window as his two younger sons entered the house. Lady J was already in the library. He'd told Fatima not to come up until he buzzed her to do so.

Now he was waiting for Touch to arrive, and the moment he did, let the party begin.

Chapter Nineteen

Touch got to the house on 68th Street ten minutes after his brothers, thanks to the woman in the parking garage who'd attempted to detain him. He didn't care that he was late. He didn't care about anything much anymore. Except for Camryn, and who knew if she was even his.

Irena could've told him, but Irena was no longer around to answer his questions.

Who would have thought that one week could totally change a person's life? His business was back on track. His personal life was pure shit.

The butler opened the front door, and he walked straight through to the library.

Lady J Bentley was sitting stiffly on one of the leather couches while Famous and Krush stood by the window. Krush immediately came over to greet him. "Tough night, huh?" Krush said in a low voice. "Did you get any sleep?"

"Not much," he replied, noticing Famous over by the window and wondering if his younger brother would have the balls to speak to him. "Where's Red?" He turned to Lady J and repeated the question.

She shrugged in a noncommittal way. "I'm sure he'll be here." Then she added, "In the future, your father and I will be going our separate ways. I thought I'd tell you before you read it in one of the columns."

Krush raised his eyebrows. "When did this happen?"

"You know what Red's like. He was always a selfish man, never cared about anyone except himself. I can't change him; no one can."

This did not exactly answer Krush's question, but he figured he'd let it go.

Lady J was no prize. She walked around as if she had a poker shoved up her Chanel-clad ass.

"Where is he?" Touch asked impatiently. "If this is a repeat performance of the other day, I'm leaving, and this time I will not be coming back."

"Ha!" Red boomed, appearing in the doorway. "Didn't expect me to make it, huh? Well, here I am. Good morning to all of you."

The old man seemed particularly cheerful as if he'd recently been privy to some excellent news. He was dressed for the occasion in a blue pin-striped suit, crisp white shirt, and bright red tie. At seventy-nine, he still had a full head of iron-grey hair, and today, it was plastered back in what he obviously considered a fetching style. His faded blue eyes were alert and crafty, while a very pleased-with-himself smile hovered on his thin lips.

Red Bentley was obviously in a very good mood indeed.

Touch Bentley was not. "Why are we here?" Touch demanded, surreptitiously cracking his knuckles.

"Patience," Red replied. "That's a quality you've never possessed." He cleared his throat, then turned his attention to Lady J. "Where are the refreshments, woman? Call the maid, for God's sake."

Lady J threw him a cool look. "I am no longer running this house," she said frostily. "Or perhaps you chose to forget that."

Ignoring her, Red picked up the phone and buzzed the kitchen, ordering coffee, tea, soft drinks, and cookies to be sent up immediately. "I enjoy a cookie in the morning," he announced as if anyone cared.

Krush stepped forward. "While you're enjoying your cookie, I have a flight to catch," he said. "You mentioned over the phone something about the true story behind my mother's plane crash. What did you mean by that?"

Von Diesel

"Christ!" Red grumbled. "Don't any of you have any goddamn manners? I called this meeting in my house, and I will conduct the order in which it takes place."

"Order?" Touch questioned. "I didn't realize we were in a boardroom."

"There will be things I say today that concern all of you," Red said. "If you want to hear them, sit down and shut up." He picked up the phone again and buzzed somewhere in the house. "Get up here, now!" he commanded.

"I thought I should inform you that I'm arranging Sadiya's funeral for early next week," Touch said. "For Camryn's sake, I'd appreciate it if you could show some respect and be there. I presume you do know that four days ago, Sadiya was brutally murdered?"

"How could I not know?" Red rasped. "It's all over the goddamn newspapers. Including my photo and a bad one at that."

Standing by the window, Famous didn't move. He regretted comparing Touch to this despicable human being, this psychologically flawed excuse for a father. It was no surprise Red had managed to turn Sukari into a pathetic drunk. She was the only one to have survived the horror of being married to such an abusive bully.

He had a strong urge to leave while he could. But something kept him there, a need to hear exactly what the old man had to say.

"I'm going to be eighty in two weeks," Red announced. "Eighty years young." He chuckled at his lame attempt at humor. "Never thought of myself as old, and I'm sure you'll all be delighted to hear that I'm healthy as a goddamn thirty-year-old. I took a physical, and I might not look it, but my body is stronger than it's ever been. Good peasant genes that were inherited from my dumbass father, the loser granddaddy

200

you were lucky enough never to know." He paused to light up a dark-colored cigarette, indulged in a short coughing fit, then continued, "I'll start with you, Touch, my eldest son. My eldest moron. You're not that smart. You just think you are. However, you managed to build yourself a mini-empire–an empire I almost took away from you with a couple of well-placed phone calls." Once again, he chuckled. "You must've learned something from me, 'cause you managed to save your ass by calling in the goddamn Japs."

"No thanks to you," Touch said, thinking how much he'd like to smash his bigoted and egocentric father in the face.

"You got enough money," Red continued. "You don't need any from me."

"Is that what you called me here to tell me?"

"No," Red said. "Stick around. It gets a lot better than this. But first, I'll move on to Krush, who thinks he's Mr. Hollywood instead of some paid shyster with a big gambling problem."

"I'm not interested in your opinion of me," Krush said, choking back his anger and frustration. "Try telling me about my mother."

"Ah…" Red sighed. "The lovely Regina. Such a beauty. Such a sad story. Foolish of her to divorce me. If she'd stayed around, she'd still be with us today."

"What do you mean?" Krush asked, his heart pounding.

"You should've asked your step-father when he was alive," Red answered, plucking a Kleenex from a box and noisily blowing his nose. "Your mother's plane crash was no damn accident. Peter Linden, her lousy choice of a second husband, handled certain clients who could take care of anything he wanted to be done. And since Mr. Linden had the hots for some movie star tramp, it seems your mother had become an inconvenience. So, he arranged to get rid of her, freeing himself to marry the movie star, which of course he did."

"What?" Krush said, dumbstruck. "How do you know this?"

"Tough shit for Peter, though," Red continued, exhaling a stream of dark smoke into the room. "Six weeks after he married the movie star, the two of them got into a fatal car accident on their way to Palm Springs. I'm sure you heard about it." A long ominous silence. "Funny how shit turns around and hits you in the face, isn't it?"

The door opened, and two maids wheeled in a trolley of refreshments. They were followed by Fatima, who stood hesitantly in the doorway.

All eyes turned to stare at the transformation of Red's dowdy housekeeper. She was quite beautiful, in an understated way.

"You all know Fatima," Red said, beckoning her to come into the room. "Housekeeper Fatima."

She entered the library reluctantly, not sure what to expect, although it was patently obvious that Red had something in mind.

Lady J Bentley glared at her while the two maids left quickly, eager to get back to the kitchen and report what was going on. Fatima sat down on the edge of the couch, as far away from Lady J as possible.

"Now let me see," Red said, enjoying every moment he spent with his captive audience. "We've established I'm in perfect health, and that's the good news, not for you, I'm sure, but good news for me. However, I'm certain you'll all be glad to know that I am getting older, and one day I will not be around to keep a watchful eye on you." A beat. "That's a joke." Another beat. "Nobody's laughing. Too bad." He swiveled his head towards his former paramour. "Jane," he said, "I have considered your request for the exorbitant and quite ludicrous sum of thirty-five million dollars, and after no thought at all, I have deemed it unacceptable. Therefore, on the condition that you and all your possessions are out of my house by six p.m. tonight, I am prepared to generously offer you one million dollars for the time you spent boring me to death. This is a one-time offer, and I suggest you accept it. Because if you refuse it, I can assure you that I will have you forcibly removed from the premises. You can try suing me for the settlement you're after. I'll have you tied up in court for the rest of your dull life. I can promise you that you'll never see a penny, so once again, I suggest you say yes to my offer."

"You bastard!" Lady J hissed.

"Not the first time I've been called that," Red said with a nasty chuckle.

"And speaking of bastards—"

Fatima's head snapped up. "Stop!" she said.

"Excuse me?" Red retorted.

The two of them had everyone's attention.

"No. Go ahead," Lady J sneered. "It's time they heard about—"

"Shut the fuck up!" Red said menacingly, angry eyes glaring at her. "This is none of your goddamn business. You snooped into my private papers, and that cost you a lot of money, so be smart for once and stay quiet."

"Well, I—"

"Did...you...hear...me?" he said in ominously measured tones.

Lady J closed her mouth.

"Famous," Red said, turning to look at his youngest son. "How's your mother? Still drinking herself into a stupor every night?"

"You gotta figure somebody made her that way," Famous muttered, determined not to be intimidated by his bullying father.

"I suppose you're intimating that it was me," Red rasped. "Newsflash, it wasn't. Sukari was a nympho, fucked anything that had a dick. The gardener in Tuscany, the chauffeur in the South of France, two of my business acquaintances—"

"Why are you doing this?" Krush interrupted. "Does it make you feel like a big man? Because in our eyes, believe me, you're not."

"Thank you, Krush, for reminding me that I digress. I must get to the real reason we're all here." A long, meaningful pause.

"Money. Inheritance. Moola. Cash. Right, my happy little family?" The room was silent.

Famous thought about his mother and felt tears prick the back of his eyelids. Shit! Mustn't cry. No way. It wasn't manly. Red had told him that when he was three, shortly after paddling his ass with a leather belt, the sharp-edged buckle drawing blood.

"Famous," Red said. "I'm opening you a bank account. In it, I will deposit five million dollars. Can't have your brothers being so far ahead of you. Competitive spirit, that's what you need. Double the five mill in five years, and there'll be more where that came from. And if one cent is spent on drugs, you'll find the money will mysteriously vanish."

Famous found his voice. "I don't want it," he said. "You can keep your money."

"I called you a fuck-up, not a fool," Red said crisply. "You have twenty-four hours to reconsider. Talk to your brothers. They'll advise you."

Lady J stood up. "You make me sick," she said, trembling with fury.

"Everything makes you sick," Red said. "Especially sex."

"I'm leaving," she said grandly.

"I suggest you stay," Red said, holding up an authoritative hand. "I'm about to reveal exactly why I summoned you all here. Surely you don't want to miss that. You could call it a surprise ending."

"While we're playing truth games, how did my mother die?" Touch asked, determined to get to the real story. "Did somebody arrange her death too?"

"Sorry to disappoint you," Red replied calmly. "Pamela had a congenital heart problem. Died of natural causes in her sleep, leaving me to take care of you. Rather inconsiderate of her, don't you think? I sure know how to pick them, don't I?"

"You didn't take care of me," Touch said heatedly. "I had a different nanny for every day of the week. I never saw you unless it was with a leather strap in your hand. Or unless you were raping one of my girlfriends."

"Boo-hoo," Red jeered. "Poor little rich boy. If you couldn't satisfy your girlfriends, somebody had to."

Touch made a move toward Red. Krush quickly restrained him.

"Someone left their balls at home," Red taunted. "You wanna punch me out? Go ahead."

"Whatever you have to say, say it now," Krush said. "Otherwise, we're leaving."

Red nodded. "You're right. Why prolong this meeting of no great minds? And Krush, I might say, if you can conquer your gambling addiction, there's a strong possibility you could amount to something after all. I like the way you're trying to take charge here, protecting your brothers. It's quite touching."

Watching the interaction between Red and his sons, Fatima felt sick. How could there be so much tension in one room, and why did Red Bentley hate his sons with such a passion?

Thank God she'd kept Velvet away from him. Not that she'd had any choice, Red had never expressed any desire to meet his daughter. He'd seen Velvet once when she was twelve, the fateful day he'd caught her napping on his bed. After that unfortunate incident, he'd insisted she was sent away.

Fatima wondered why Red wanted her and Velvet at this meeting. When Velvet found out that Red Bentley was her father, she'd go crazy. She had always expressed her loathing of him. Fatima knew that when she discovered the truth, there would be an explosion.

"Let me get down to it," Red said, clearing his throat. "Unfortunately, in spite of my excellent physical condition, I will not be around forever. This means that I will be obliged to leave my estate to someone."

"Find a charity. We're not interested," Touch muttered.

"When I'm dead and gone, you'll change your minds," Red said. "Money has a way of making people change their minds. So, to prevent any untoward claims on my estate, I have recently made an iron-clad Will that leaves everything– and I mean everything, to your two sisters."

"Sisters?" Krush said. "We don't have sisters."

"I knew there was something I forgot to mention," Red said, enjoying every moment of his revelation. "Fatima," he ordered, "stand up and tell them about our daughter. Sorry, Lady J, I know you wanted to be the one to spit it out, but we can't always get what we want, can we?"

Lady J shot him a venomous look. She wanted to leave and call her lawyer. On the other hand, she was frightened she might miss something that she could use later.

Fatima felt exposed and vulnerable. Why was he doing this to her? After Zippy's demise, she'd kept her silence. She'd done everything Red had asked her to. To this day, she was not sure if she or Red had shot Zippy. They'd been locked in a tangle, and somehow or other, the gun had gone off. Had she pulled the trigger, or had Red? Because when Zippy slumped to the floor, the gun had thudded to the ground, and she'd never been sure who'd actually shot him.

Red had been determined to avoid any scandal. He'd immediately taken over, arranging for Zippy's body to be removed, offering Fatima a job as his housekeeper. He'd promised her room and board and a lump sum of money sometime in the future. In a veiled way, he'd threatened her that if she didn't do exactly as he suggested, Zippy's body would be found, and she'd be arrested for his murder. "Who will the cops believe?" he'd said. "A black woman or a white man? Your kid will go into the welfare system, and you'll be fucked."

Tired and scared, she'd agreed to everything. At the time, it hadn't seemed so bad, a safe haven, no more singing for money to keep the bills paid. Red switched Velvet to an expensive private school in Manhattan and paid for any incidentals. Fatima had comforted herself with the thought that Velvet was getting a far better education than she could have afforded to give her.

And now, almost ten years later, here she was sitting in Red Bentley's library while he prepared to reveal that he was Velvet's father because he felt like it. Yes, she thought. Red Bentley is as bad as everyone says he is. Cruel, arrogant, a manipulative bully. How much longer could she put up with him?

She was damned if she was going to tell them about Velvet. Let him be the one to do so if he was so anxious for them to know.

"Seems Fatima has lost her voice," Red said. "She looks pretty today, doesn't she? Cleans up nicely. You should've seen her when she was singing all my favorite songs. She was quite a beauty then. A black beauty." Another chuckle. "Can't blame a man for dipping into a chocolate sundae for a change. But disappointingly, Brown Sugar tricked me and got herself pregnant. So, being the man I am, I took her and the baby in. And in case your fertile minds are wondering, tests were done, and the child is mine. A man can never be too sure."

Fatima felt like laughing in his face. *Took her and the baby in. Really?* Velvet was almost ten years old when they came to live with him, and the only reason that happened was because of Zippy's demise and the confusion over who might have shot him.

"Speak up, Fatima," Red ordered. "We're all waiting. What's the girl's name?"

"I can tell you're as close to her as you were to us," Krush said, vaguely remembering that when Fatima had first come to work for Red, he'd seen a scrawny little kid running around a couple of times. "You don't even know her name."

"If I've got a sister, I want to meet her," Famous said.

"Why?" Red questioned, adding a succinct, "Oh, I get it. I told you she's getting all my money, so why not make friends?"

"You said sisters," Touch interrupted. "What other surprises do you have for us?"

"One that you're not going to like," Red said, rubbing his hands together.

"It's about Camryn."

"What about her?"

"Sadiya and I were very close, you know."

"No, you weren't."

"Yes. We were."

"What about Camryn?"

"Sorry, Touch, to be the one to tell you, but Sadiya and I were closer than you thought. Camryn is my daughter."

Touch shook his head, convinced he was in the middle of some hideous nightmare.

"What did you say?" he managed.

"Lie down with dogs, and you get fleas. Marry whores, and you get what you deserve. Didn't I teach you anything?"

Before anyone could say a word, there was a noisy commotion outside the library, and the door burst open.

Into the room came Detective Banks, his female partner, and two uniformed cops. They were followed by an outraged butler.

"What the hell is going on?" Red bellowed. "Who are you, people? And what the hell are you doing, bursting into my house like this?"

"We have an arrest warrant, Mr. Bentley," Detective Banks said, waving the warrant in front of him.

"A warrant?" Red shouted his craggy face darkening. "For which one of my useless sons?"

"For you, Mr. Bentley," Detective Banks said, his words slow and forceful. "I am placing you under arrest for the murder of Sadiya Bentley."

Chapter Twenty

After Red's revelations and subsequent arrest, somehow
or other Krush found himself in charge. Touch was a mess.
Famous was in shock. And Fatima was hysterical. She ap-
pealed to Krush to find Velvet before the press discovered
that Red Bentley had an illegitimate daughter.

"Tell me where she is, and I'll get her back here," Krush
promised.

Fatima was vague. All she knew was the name of the hotel Velvet was staying at in L.A.

With the small amount of information he had, and a photo
of Velvet supplied by Fatima, Krush called Chi-rone in L.A.,
e-mailed him the photo and dispatched his assistant to Shutters to find her.

Chi-rone, being the diligent person he was, got to Shutters just as Velvet and Tristin were about to step into a limo
on their way to Tristin's plane.

Chi-rone was able to convince Velvet that her mother
needed to see her urgently. Tristin reluctantly understood,
and instead of flying to Cabo, they flew directly to New York.

"I have no clue what's going down," Tristin said to Velvet when his plane landed in New York, "but whatever it is,
LL, you know I got your back."

When Fatima told Velvet the truth, her world shattered.
Red Bentley was her father. Red Bentley, a man she loathed.
Red Bentley, the man who banished her from his house and
forced her mother to work as a maid.

"He didn't force me," Fatima sighed, leaving out the part
about Zippy. "I chose to work for him."

"And now he's been arrested for murder?" Velvet said,
horrified.

"I'm sorry, Velvet. I know I should've told you about Red
before. I…I don't know why I didn't."

Velvet ran straight to Tristin. He was the only person she felt she could trust.

"You're getting away," he told her. "Out of New York. Out of this whole scene. I got a house on Paradise Island in the Bahamas. A house, recording studio, the works. I already talked to Parker, and he's gonna fly down there with you. The two of you are gonna work on your music."

"Why are you doing this for me?" she asked. "You're not getting anything out of it."

"Oh, yes, I am, babe," he said, giving her the look. "I'm getting me a future star, so don't you be letting me down."

***

Famous immediately called Shemika and asked her to meet him at Eddie's place. She did so, and he told her everything before she heard it on the news.

She was there for him, in spite of the fit she knew her mother would throw.

"What about Touch?" she asked. "Shouldn't we be with him?"

"Yeah, if he wants us," Famous agreed.

But they couldn't reach Touch. He was already in his car on his way to Montauk.

When he arrived, he hugged Camryn for a long time, then sat in the garden with her playing games. She'd already lost her mother: he was determined she wouldn't lose him too.

***

Krush waited until Red was released on ten million dollars bail, then flew back to L.A. and onto Vegas. Chilly Rose was on the outs with her fiancé, so he had a wedding to cancel and a debt to pay. He took care of both.

In a few days, he decided he'd fly back to New York, mainly to check on his brothers. It was a tough time for all of them, and he wanted to make sure everyone was okay.

Since when had he become the responsible one in the family?

He was a lawyer, looking after people went with the territory.

The trial of Red Bentley for the murder of Sadiya Bentley would've been huge. A mega-billionaire stabbing his son's wife to death in a jealous frenzy when he'd discovered she entertained other lovers was a story made in heaven.

However, it did not come to pass. Arrested and released on ten million dollars bail, Red Bentley suffered a massive heart attack and expired two weeks after his initial arrest.

Detective Banks was unhappy not to get his day in court. After all, he was the one who had painstakingly put it together. Who else would've suspected a powerful man such as Red Bentley?

He'd started to wonder about Red when, right at the beginning of his investigation, the billionaire had refused to see him.

Flag number one. His daughter-in-law had been murdered, yet Red Bentley did not want to answer any questions about his son's wife. Why?

Flag number two. He'd looked Red Bentley up on the internet and found a wealth of material, including his interest in swords and daggers. Apparently, he had quite a collection. The coroner had stated that Sadiya had been stabbed with some kind of old-fashioned dagger.

Flag number three. According to the desk clerk in her building and two parking attendants in the underground garage, Sadiya had entertained three men on a regular basis. One was a reclusive elderly man, who always arrived bundled up in a scarf, a hat pulled low over his forehead and come rain or shine, black-out sunglasses. The desk clerk recalled seeing him late Sunday night, around the time Sadiya was probably killed. The man usually arrived in a town car, always with a different driver.

Detective Banks had built his entire career on gut feelings. He was good, very good. And he'd had a gut feeling about Red Bentley right from the start. He didn't know why; it was just one of those things. Because of those feelings, he'd followed every lead. There were fingerprints on Sadiya's body, and while he was researching Red Bentley, he'd discovered there was a time when Red had decided to buy a casino in Vegas. He'd needed a gaming license. The gaming board needed his fingerprints.

It was a match. And Detective Banks had no doubt the other DNA samples would be a match too. Sperm, hair, skin. It was all there, and one of the parking attendants was able to identify Red.

Regarding Sadiya's mother, Irena, Detective Banks had no gut feeling. But once Red was under arrest, he turned his attention to solving Irena's murder. It shouldn't be that difficult.

He started with Sadiya's Russian phone book.

Von Diesel

Epilogue
One Year Later

Sometimes careers take a long time to take off—other times, it's instant stardom. Like an incandescent shooting star, the combination of Velvet's looks and her untapped talent catapulted her into the second category.

Her first CD made it to the top of the charts within weeks of hitting the stores. From an unknown cover girl on *White Cool* magazine, she was suddenly Velvet, the latest female singing sensation. The critics loved her.

Entertainment Weekly wrote, "Exotically beautiful with a voice to match. Velvet is the new Alicia Keys/Norah Jones/female Usher combination. Her sultry, soulful style will stop you dead. Her CD, Revelations, is just that. A true revelation of the highest order. Download *Married Man*, a sassy, poignant commentary on not making out with married men. Velvet is destined to go far."

Malshonda read her the review over the phone from Cleveland, where she was on tour with Slick Jimmy. Surprisingly, Malshonda's relationship with Slick Jimmy had endured. And although Malshonda was not yet Mrs. Slick Jimmy, she had given birth to a gorgeous baby boy they'd named, much to Aretha's horror, Baby Rap. Malshonda was happy. That was the main thing.

"Unbelievable, girl!" Malshonda enthused. "What does Tristin have to say?"

"I'm not sure he's seen it yet," Velvet answered vaguely.

She didn't want to mention that she hardly ever saw Tristin anymore.

After their aborted trip to Cabo and the following dramas, he'd sent her off to the Bahamas with Parker and totally backed away from anything personal between them.

At first, she'd thought his absence was just temporary, but after a while, she realized he was all-business towards her. Friendly, encouraging, but all business. She couldn't figure it out.

"Call him up," Malshonda insisted. "Tell him to send someone out to buy the magazine. You know how many extra copies of your CD is gonna sell?"

"I'm on my way to the airport."

"Going where?"

"L.A. I'm appearing on *The Tonight Show*."

"Bring it, girl!" Malshonda said, impressed. "You're a star!"

Velvet hung up the phone. She didn't feel like a star; she felt very alone. Suddenly becoming the center of attention was a scary place to be.

Oh, yes, she was surrounded by minders, thanks to Tristin, but she was still alone. All the managers, producers, and publicists in the world didn't make up for not having that one special person by her side.

When she'd first arrived at Tristin's house in the Bahamas, she'd been so sure that, within weeks, he'd be there with her. After L.A., she'd felt as if they were just about to embark on an adventure. But no, he had never come. He called occasionally, and Parker assured her he was happy with the demo tapes of her new songs and the arrangements they were working on.

After a couple of months, she decided to call Tristin and ask him if it was okay if her boyfriend came to visit. "If that's what you want," Tristin said over the phone.

She hung up, furious. That was it, no more thinking about Tristin. It was quite clear that he wasn't thinking about her. He was busy doing other things, other girls. Screw him. She convinced herself that she didn't care anymore.

Keylan arrived for a week and left after three days. She tried to let him down easy, but as far as she was concerned, the thrill was definitely gone.

The night he left, she sat down and wrote *Married Man*, a farewell ode to Tristin.

Lately, she'd been thinking a lot about calling her mother and reconnecting. After finding out that Red Bentley was her father, she hadn't wanted anything to do with Fatima. She hadn't wanted anything to do with any of the Bentley family either. Although deep down, she knew she was being unreasonable. It wasn't their fault that Red had turned out to be her father.

Still, she was sure they must hate her, the illegitimate half-black sister who was due to inherit half of Red's fortune when she hit twenty-five.

Not that she had any intention of taking his money. She didn't want it, it wasn't hers, and she refused to give it any serious thought.

*** *** ***

There were three murders in Manhattan over a long hot weekend. One was a mugging that went too far. The second was a shooting. And the third was a statuesque Russian call-girl.

Detective Banks stood in the hotel room where she had been discovered by a now hysterical maid. He stared down at the woman's naked body sprawled half-off, half-on the bed. She was a beauty all right, with flaming-red hair and whiter than white skin.

Someone had strangled her with their bare hands, and the bruises on her neck were already a deep purple.

Detective Banks remembered the woman from his investigation of Sadiya Bentley's mother's murder, Irena, shot in her tiny apartment in Brighton Beach.

After some fine detective work, he'd unearthed a ring of jewelry thieves connected to the Russian mob. Sadiya Bentley had been involved somehow, along with her sometime lover, Alex Pinchinoff, a very nasty piece of work.

Several months previously, when Detective Banks had arrived at Alex Pinchinoff's apartment to question the man, the red-haired woman had answered the door. She'd been quite obliging, told him she was Alex's girlfriend, and that Alex was in Europe on business. It hadn't taken him long to find out exactly who she was. Isha Parker: a working call-girl.

Detective Banks had been unable to prove that Alex Pinchinoff had had anything to do with Irena's murder, and one of Alex's henchmen had taken the fall. Igor, a weasel of a man, confessed to shooting Irena on nobody's orders.

Right. Nobody's orders. Sure.

Detective Banks had it figured out that Alex Pinchinoff had sent the man to recover Sadiya's box of cash and loose stones, which he thought Irena had. After recovering the box, he was to kill her so she couldn't talk. The man had killed her all right, without recovering anything.

Ever since then, Detective Banks had kept a watchful eye on Alex Pinchinoff. He'd nail him for something. Eventually.

Detective Banks stared at the redhead's neck.

Perhaps she'd known too much.

Perhaps Alex had dispatched her himself.

There were bruises on her neck and fingerprints...

Detective Banks felt the hairs on the back of his neck stand up. He had a gut feeling...

***

Eventually, Krush had talked Famous into accepting the money Red had left him. "Why not?" Krush had said. "You're with a girl who will inherit a fortune one day, so take advantage of five mill in the bank. After the way we were raised, you kinda deserve it, little bro."

After thinking it through and discussing it with Shemika, Famous agreed. It seemed foolish not to accept it.

So, he took the money and purchased a loft in Tribeca. He also hooked up with a top modeling agency, and after the Ciccone ads appeared, he began getting excellent bookings, plus a couple of major endorsement deals, one to be the face of Dolce and Gabbana cologne. Quite a coup.

Shemika kept her job at Ciccone, and after a while, she sold her apartment and moved in with Famous.

Her mother was beyond furious. Nancy rushed over to Grandma Poppy's and informed the old lady that under no account was she to leave Shemika any money.

Grandma Poppy was quite amused. She told Nancy to calm down and go away. "My money goes wherever I want it to go, and it's certainly not going to you, Nancy. Dear, you have more than enough as it is."

Grandma Poppy couldn't wait to tell Shemika all about her meeting with Nancy. They both had a good laugh, and later that night, Shemika brought Famous over for dinner.

Grandma Poppy was quite entranced. "This one's a keeper, dear," she informed her granddaughter.

Shemika smiled. "I think so."

"Don't let him get away."

"Got a feeling he doesn't want to, Grams."

After several months of happy togetherness, Famous suggested that it might be a great idea if they got married.

Shemika demurred. As much as she loved him, she wasn't quite sure she was ready. But after several weeks of discussing it, they decided to take out a wedding license just in case. A week later, they got married in City Hall. As far as Shemika was concerned, it was the perfect way to do it.

***

Touch kept Camryn. Both Famous and Krush agreed it was for the best not to tell the little girl anything until she was older and could understand.

Red Bentley was headline news for many months. Then, gradually, people moved on. The information about Red's two illegitimate daughters fortunately never made it to the newspapers or rags. It was a family secret, and it would stay that way.

The brothers agreed to sell the house on 68th Street. It was owned by a trust in their names. An asset Red had managed to overlook. Or maybe he had meant them to have something.

Once they'd sold the house, they made a substantial payment to Lady J Bentley to secure her silence. Fatima had already sworn she would never say a word, but since Red had only left her what they considered a small amount in his will, they compensated her too.

Touch threw himself back into his business, ignoring the scandal that swirled around him. His multi-million-dollar commercial building project was almost completed. The Japanese bankers were so delighted that they wished to invest in any other projects he might bring them. Touch had plans for several new towering apartment buildings to be built near the river. The Japanese assured him that money was no problem.

Socially he was invited everywhere. He was rich, successful, and single, so every New York hostess had him on their A-list.

So far, he had not met anyone he cared to spend time with. But it would happen. He was confident that there was someone out there who'd be right for him.

***

Free at last, Fatima left the house on 68th Street and moved in with her sister for a while. Velvet wasn't speaking to her, but Velvet was still in touch with Aretha, so Fatima felt that at least she had some connection to her daughter.

One afternoon, out shopping for groceries, she stopped off at a used record store she'd been meaning to visit. The place was full of old-time LPs with glamorous shots of stars like Aretha Franklin and Diana Ross on the sleeves. Flipping through the albums, Fatima recalled her days singing at Gloria's and how much she'd loved it. She wondered if the club was still there and if Gloria was looking for a somewhat rusty jazz singer.

Why not? she thought. She could still sing, she looked okay, and she wasn't even forty, so why not? Shivering with excitement just thinking about it, she chose a Billie Holiday album and took it up to the counter.

"This is out on CD," the young girl behind the counter informed her.

"That's not what you're supposed to say in a store that sells old records," the owner of the store said, emerging from an office in the back. He was tall and nice-looking, very black and very familiar.

"Leon?" Fatima questioned, recognizing him immediately.

"Fatima?" he said, his face lighting up.

She nodded.

He beamed.

It had been twelve years, but within two weeks, they were living together again.

***

It took several arduous months for Krush to painstakingly restore his house to its pristine state, but once it was done, it was worth it. Then, a few weeks later, he received a call from Kareema.

"I am in Hollywood," she announced in her charming accent. "I am doing big movie. I play the Italian girl." Surprise. Surprise.

"You called me once, a while ago," he said. "Then I never heard from you again."

"I didn't want to bother you, Krush, with your family, how you say, difficulties? My English good now, sì?"

"Yes," he answered, smiling because he was genuinely pleased to hear from her.

A few days previously, sitting in his office with Chilly Rose, currently engaged to a raunchy rock and roller, the sexy young singer had leaned across his desk and said, "Like, what you need, dude, is some fun. You're getting so freaking serious in your old age."

Old age indeed! He was only thirty-three.

Now here she was. Kareema. On the phone. And she represented fun with a capital F.

"How about dinner tonight?" he suggested.

"Is good," she said.

"Is very good," he agreed. "Where are you staying?"

"L'Hermitage."

"I'll pick you up. Eight o'clock suits you?"

"Good, Krush. Very Good."

That was a few months ago, and they'd been together ever since. Nothing serious. Just fun.

***

Sitting in her dressing room, waiting to appear on *The Tonight Show*, Velvet picked up the phone and called her mother. She'd heard all about Fatima reconnecting with Leon, and she was pleased for her. She hadn't seen Leon since she was seven, but she remembered him as a great guy. He was always looking out for her.

A man answered the phone.

"Leon?" she said tentatively.

"Is that my baby girl?" he responded warmly. "My partner in long walks through the park and all those visits to the zoo?"

"Yes, it is," she said, smiling. "And guess what? I'm all grown-up."

"So, I noticed. Your mama has that photo of you from the front of your CD all around our apartment."

"I'm really glad you and Mama are back together," she said, genuinely meaning it.

"You're glad," he said fervently. "How do you think I feel after all those years without her?"

"Well, you left."

"She threw me out, baby girl, 'cause I wasn't in a marrying mood."

"Are you in a marriage mood now?" Velvet asked, still smiling.

"You bet I am. Only your mama ain't."

"Is she around?"

"Hold on. She's sure gonna be happy to hear from you."

Penny, one of the record company's publicists assigned to look after her, came into the dressing room.

"Give me a minute," Velvet said, waving her away.

"Sure," Penny said. "I'll go check out the Green Room, see who the other guests are."

Velvet waited patiently for her mother to pick up. Speaking to Leon had summoned up a lot of memories. She remembered the three of them sitting around listening to Leon's record collection. They'd made sure she was exposed to the best, Marvin Gaye, Aretha Franklin, Al Green. Great early influences. Then there were the special nights when Leon and Mama had sung their duets for her. They'd seemed so happy together.

"Velvet? Is that really you?"

Her mama's sweet voice, and she wanted to hug her because it couldn't have been easy, and now it was definitely time to put the past to rest. "Yes, Mama," she said softly, "It's me."

**

Shemika and Famous were sitting in the back of a limo on their way to *The Tonight Show*. Krush had invited them as they were visiting L.A., and Kareema was appearing on the show.

"I am so not jealous," Shemika said.

"You're sure?" Famous asked.

"Why would I be? I like her."

"You do?"

"Well, I did when I met her. Granted, that was over a year ago, but I'm sure she can't have changed."

"I liked her too."

"Now, wait a minute."

"Hey," he said innocently, "nothing wrong with liking someone. And now she's with Krush, so everything's cool. Right?"

"You bet right," Shemika said sternly. "Let us not forget you are a married man, Mr. Bentley."

"Yes, Mrs. Bentley."

"You have responsibilities."

"I certainly do."

They both grinned and exchanged a hug.

"I suppose she's considered a movie star now," Shemika remarked. "Not after one movie, which hasn't even opened yet." "She's beautiful enough to be one," Shemika said wistfully.

"You're more beautiful," Famous insisted.

"Liar!" Shemika said, blushing.

"I mean it."

She glanced at their driver, sitting ramrod straight behind the wheel. "How do you close the privacy panel in this car?" she asked Famous, lowering her voice.

"Huh?"

"Can you close it?"

"Oh, I get it," he said, leaning forward to press the button. "We're gonna make out in the back of a limo. it's our Hollywood thing, kinda rite of passage."

"Honestly, Famous!"

"What?" he said, reaching for her as the dark glass slid into place, cutting them off from the driver. "Don't you wanna make out?"

"Yes."

"So?"

"First, I have something to tell you."

"Go ahead."

"We're pregnant," she whispered.

"Come again?"

"Pregnant. You, Mr. Bentley, are about to become a daddy."

"Holy shit!" he said, breaking out an enormous grin.

"Daddy Famous."

"Yes," she said softly, kissing him. "Daddy Famous."

***

Penny, the publicist, returned to the dressing room exactly five minutes later.

"Gotta go, Mama," Velvet said into the phone. "Don't forget to watch." She clicked off.

"Nervous?" Penny asked.

"I'm trying not to be."

"The rehearsals went well," Penny said briskly. "Kevin Eubanks seems charming."

"Hmm..." Velvet murmured, happy that she'd had a really nice conversation with her mother. They'd arranged to get together as soon as she got back to New York. She couldn't wait. And she'd see Leon, how great was that?

"There's a guy in the Green Room who wants to stop by and say hello," Penny said, helping herself to a Diet Coke.

"Who?" Velvet asked, adjusting her leather gown.

"He's here with his girlfriend, Kareema. She's a guest on the show."

"Who is he, Penny?"

"Uh, Krush Bentley. Says you know him." Krush Bentley. This was a surprise.

She was silent for a moment, trying to decide what to do. Well, since she was mending bridges, why not see him?

"Okay." She sighed. "Where is he?"

"I'll go get him," Penny said. "Unless you want to make the trek to the Green Room and meet him there."

"No. Bring him here."

"Sure," Penny said.

This was turning out to be some night–first her mom, now Krush Bentley. Over the past year, she'd often thought about her three half-brothers and the little sister she'd never met. Somehow or other, she'd locked herself into a mindset that they wanted nothing to do with her.

Now Krush Bentley was here at *The Tonight Show*, and he was asking to see her.

She attempted to compose herself while Penny went to fetch him. What was she supposed to say to him? It was such an insane situation.

Krush burst into her dressing room, not giving her a chance to say anything. "You know, this is ridiculous," he said. "And I want to start right here–right now–to get to know you."

Penny, immediately behind him, rolled her eyes and mouthed, "Who-is this-guy? Shall-I-get-rid-of-him?"

"That's okay, Penny," Velvet said quickly. "Give us some privacy." Penny frowned, backed out, and shut the door.

"So," Krush said, "we're blood. Unfortunately, it's Red's blood, but we can get over that."

"We can?" she said unsurely.

"Yes," he said firmly. "And you should know, up-front, that this is not about the money."

"I don't want the money," she said. "I never did."

"Well, it's yours, and Camryn's to do whatever you like with."

"I'd like to give it away to different charities who need it more than I do. I can make my own money; I don't want his."

"Fine with me."

"Yes?" she said tentatively.

"It would drive Red crazy, so I'm all for it."

"Good."

"Then that's taken care of. And now, in the future, I'd like to get to know the sister I never had. Can we do that?"

She smiled, a small smile, but it was a start. "I think I can definitely say I'd love it."

As soon as Krush left, Penny put her head around the door. "Okay, to come back?"

"Sure," Velvet said.

Penny was dying to find out who Krush was, but she managed to restrain herself, as Velvet didn't seem in a talkative mood. However, she couldn't stop herself saying, "Handsome guy." Velvet nodded.

"I just found out that Jay Leno might stop by the dressing room," Penny said. "He usually tries to greet his guests personally before they go on. Oh, great! Something else to make her feel nervous."

"Do you mind if I take a little alone time?" Velvet murmured.

"Absolutely," Penny said. "Get your head together. You've got at least an hour before you go on. I'm on my cell. Call when you need me." Velvet nodded again, and once more, Penny took off.

As soon as she was alone, Velvet checked out her reflection in the full-length mirror. Various stylists had attempted to change her look, but she'd insisted on keeping it simple. Her hair, long and dark, fell past her shoulders. Her make-up was sexy and seductive, and she'd elected to wear the Versace leather dress from her L.A. photoshoot with Chip. The moment she'd started making money, she'd tracked it down and bought it. She referred to it as her lucky dress.

Five minutes later, there was a knock on the dressing room door. She prepared herself to meet Mr. Leno. Jay Leno. The Jay Leno, a man she and Malshonda had grown up watching on TV.

"Come in," she called.

And he did. Only it wasn't Jay Leno. It was Tristin. And he was carrying a huge bowl of purple and white orchids. "Delivery," he said, cool and casual. "Where do you want them?"

"Tristin!" she gasped, totally surprised. "What are you doing here?"

He placed the orchids on a table. "You're my artist. You record for my label. So, I kinda figured that I should be the one to tell you that your CD hits number one next week. You're knocking off Eminem and Mariah Carey, so I guess we can safely say you've made it. Here," he said, thrusting a large manilla envelope at her. "Read this."

"Another contract?" she asked, struggling to remain in control of her emotions.

"Kinda. Sorta," he said casually. "Read it."

"Not now," she said, because she didn't need this, she was nervous enough about appearing on Leno.

"Now." A long beat. A long look. "I'm asking nicely."

She stared at him for a moment. He was still as handsome as ever, with his close-cropped hair and Bentley stud earring. Tonight, he had on a white suit, white silk T, thin black leather belt with a Bentley buckle, and the usual Nikes. Tristin had a style that was all his own.

"If you insist," she said, tearing open the envelope.

"Thanks," he said.

"What is this?" she asked, after a few moments of reading.

"You don't get it?"

"No."

"A signed, sealed, and witnessed agreement between me and Tash."

"Your wife?"

"Now you're getting there," he said, giving her a long intimate look.

"How come you're showing it to me?" she asked, quite puzzled.

"It's a property agreement dividing up our assets."

"Yes?"

"You see, when I married Tash, I didn't think it was cool to start asking her to sign a prenup and all that shit. So now that I'm getting a divorce, I wanted it all worked out up-front. I'm giving her half of everything. That way, she'll let me walk away clean."

"She will?"

"Oh, yeah. No hassle. No bad vibes."

"Can I ask why you're doing this?"

"You really mean to tell me you don't know?" he said quizzically.

"No. I don't know," she said, thinking Tristin was getting a divorce!

"It's all because of you, baby."

"It is?" she asked, feeling light-headed and slightly breathless.

"Yeah. I kinda got your message."

"Um…what message would that be?"

"That I couldn't play hit it and run with you. That you, LL, are a total commitment. So…if you're still interested, I'm making myself available. And these papers prove I ain't talking whack. We together on this?"

"Yes, we're together," she whispered, trying to stop the shaking in her heart.

"Then it's all good. And I was thinking that after you're through with the show tonight, my plane is waiting, and so is Cabo. It seems like a plan to take up where we left off." A long beat. "You know what I'm saying? You and me, Cabo?"

"Separate rooms?" she teased.

"No freaking way."

"Then, Tristin," she said, her spirits soaring, "it's on."

The End

Von Diesel

Lock Down Publications and Ca$h Presents assisted
publishing packages.

BASIC PACKAGE $499
Editing
Cover Design
Formatting

UPGRADED PACKAGE $800
Typing
Editing
Cover Design
Formatting

ADVANCE PACKAGE $1,200
Typing
Editing
Cover Design
Formatting
Copyright registration
Proofreading
Upload book to Amazon

LDP SUPREME PACKAGE $1,500
Typing
Editing
Cover Design
Formatting
Copyright registration
Proofreading
Set up Amazon account

Upload book to Amazon
Advertise on LDP Amazon and Facebook page

***Other services available upon request. Additional charges may apply
Lock Down Publications
P.O. Box 944
Stockbridge, GA 30281-9998
Phone # 470 303-9761

Von Diesel

Submission Guideline

Submit the first three chapters of your completed manuscript to ldpsubmissions@gmail.com, subject line: Your book's title. The manuscript must be in a .doc file and sent as an attachment. Document should be in Times New Roman, double spaced and in size 12 font. Also, provide your synopsis and full contact information. If sending multiple submissions, they must each be in a separate email.

Have a story but no way to send it electronically? You can still submit to LDP/Ca$h Presents. Send in the first three chapters, written or typed, of your completed manuscript to:

LDP: Submissions Dept
Po Box 944
Stockbridge, Ga 30281

DO NOT send original manuscript. Must be a duplicate.

Provide your synopsis and a cover letter containing your full contact information.

Thanks for considering LDP and Ca$h Presents.

Von Diesel

NEW RELEASES

THE STREETS WILL NEVER CLOSE
by K'AJJI
MONEY IN THE GRAVE 3 by MAR-
TELL "TROUBLESOME" BOLDEN
BETRAYAL OF A THUG by FRE$H
THE STREETS WILL TALK by
YOLANDA MOORE
THE COCAINE PRINCESS by KING
RIO
THE BILLIONAIRE BENTLEYS by
VON DIESEL

Von Diesel

The Billionaire Bentleys

Coming Soon from Lock Down Publications/Ca$h Presents

BLOOD OF A BOSS **VI**

SHADOWS OF THE GAME II

TRAP BASTARD II

By **Askari**

LOYAL TO THE GAME **IV**

By **T.J. & Jelissa**

IF TRUE SAVAGE **VIII**

MIDNIGHT CARTEL IV

DOPE BOY MAGIC IV

CITY OF KINGZ III

NIGHTMARE ON SILENT AVE II

THE PLUG OF LIL MEXICO II

By **Chris Green**

BLAST FOR ME **III**

A SAVAGE DOPEBOY III

CUTTHROAT MAFIA III

DUFFLE BAG CARTEL VII

HEARTLESS GOON VI

By **Ghost**

A HUSTLER'S DECEIT III

KILL ZONE II

BAE BELONGS TO ME III

By **Aryanna**

KING OF THE TRAP III

By **T.J. Edwards**

GORILLAZ IN THE BAY V

Von Diesel

3X KRAZY III

STRAIGHT BEAST MODE II

De'Kari

KINGPIN KILLAZ IV

STREET KINGS III

PAID IN BLOOD III

CARTEL KILLAZ IV

DOPE GODS III

Hood Rich

SINS OF A HUSTLA II

ASAD

RICH $AVAGE II

By Martell Troublesome Bolden

YAYO V

Bred In The Game 2

S. Allen

CREAM III

THE STREETS WILL TALK II

By Yolanda Moore

SON OF A DOPE FIEND III

HEAVEN GOT A GHETTO II

By Renta

LOYALTY AIN'T PROMISED III

By Keith Williams

I'M NOTHING WITHOUT HIS LOVE II

SINS OF A THUG II

TO THE THUG I LOVED BEFORE II

The Billionaire Bentleys

IN A HUSTLER I TRUST II

By Monet Dragun

QUIET MONEY IV

EXTENDED CLIP III

THUG LIFE IV

By **Trai'Quan**

THE STREETS MADE ME IV

By **Larry D. Wright**

IF YOU CROSS ME ONCE II

By **Anthony Fields**

THE STREETS WILL NEVER CLOSE III

By K'ajji

HARD AND RUTHLESS III

KILLA KOUNTY III

By Khufu

MONEY GAME III

By Smoove Dolla

JACK BOYS VS DOPE BOYS II

A GANGSTA'S QUR'AN V

By Romell Tukes

MURDA WAS THE CASE II

Elijah R. Freeman

THE STREETS NEVER LET GO II

By Robert Baptiste

AN UNFORESEEN LOVE III

By **Meesha**

KING OF THE TRENCHES III

Von Diesel

by **GHOST & TRANAY ADAMS**

MONEY MAFIA II

LOYAL TO THE SOIL III

By **Jibril Williams**

QUEEN OF THE ZOO II

By **Black Migo**

THE BRICK MAN IV

THE COCAINE PRINCESS IV

By King Rio

VICIOUS LOYALTY II

By Kingpen

A GANGSTA'S PAIN II

By J-Blunt

CONFESSIONS OF A JACKBOY III

By Nicholas Lock

GRIMEY WAYS II

By Ray Vinci

KING KILLA II

By Vincent "Vitto" Holloway

BETRAYAL OF A THUG II

By Fre$h

Available Now

RESTRAINING ORDER **I & II**
By **CA$H & Coffee**
LOVE KNOWS NO BOUNDARIES **I II & III**
By **Coffee**
RAISED AS A GOON I, II, III & IV
BRED BY THE SLUMS I, II, III
BLAST FOR ME I & II
ROTTEN TO THE CORE I II III
A BRONX TALE I, II, III
DUFFLE BAG CARTEL I II III IV V VI
HEARTLESS GOON I II III IV V
A SAVAGE DOPEBOY I II
DRUG LORDS I II III
CUTTHROAT MAFIA I II
KING OF THE TRENCHES
By **Ghost**
LAY IT DOWN **I & II**
LAST OF A DYING BREED I II
BLOOD STAINS OF A SHOTTA I & II III
By **Jamaica**
LOYAL TO THE GAME I II III
LIFE OF SIN I, II III
By **TJ & Jelissa**
BLOODY COMMAS I & II

Von Diesel

SKI MASK CARTEL I II & III

KING OF NEW YORK I II,III IV V

RISE TO POWER I II III

COKE KINGS I II III IV V

BORN HEARTLESS I II III IV

KING OF THE TRAP I II

By **T.J. Edwards**

IF LOVING HIM IS WRONG...I & II

LOVE ME EVEN WHEN IT HURTS I II III

By **Jelissa**

WHEN THE STREETS CLAP BACK I & II III

THE HEART OF A SAVAGE I II III

MONEY MAFIA

LOYAL TO THE SOIL I II

By **Jibril Williams**

A DISTINGUISHED THUG STOLE MY HEART I II & III

LOVE SHOULDN'T HURT I II III IV

RENEGADE BOYS I II III IV

PAID IN KARMA I II III

SAVAGE STORMS I II III

AN UNFORESEEN LOVE I II

By **Meesha**

A GANGSTER'S CODE I &, II III

A GANGSTER'S SYN I II III

THE SAVAGE LIFE I II III

CHAINED TO THE STREETS I II III

BLOOD ON THE MONEY I II III

244

The Billionaire Bentleys

A GANGSTA'S PAIN

By J-Blunt

PUSH IT TO THE LIMIT

By **Bre' Hayes**

BLOOD OF A BOSS **I, II, III, IV, V**

SHADOWS OF THE GAME

TRAP BASTARD

By **Askari**

THE STREETS BLEED MURDER **I, II & III**

THE HEART OF A GANGSTA I II& III

By **Jerry Jackson**

CUM FOR ME I II III IV V VI VII VIII

An **LDP Erotica Collaboration**

BRIDE OF A HUSTLA **I II & II**

THE FETTI GIRLS **I, II& III**

CORRUPTED BY A GANGSTA I, II III, IV

BLINDED BY HIS LOVE

THE PRICE YOU PAY FOR LOVE I, II ,III

DOPE GIRL MAGIC I II III

By **Destiny Skai**

WHEN A GOOD GIRL GOES BAD

By **Adrienne**

THE COST OF LOYALTY I II III

By Kweli

A GANGSTER'S REVENGE **I II III & IV**

THE BOSS MAN'S DAUGHTERS I II III IV V

A SAVAGE LOVE **I & II**

Von Diesel

BAE BELONGS TO ME I II
A HUSTLER'S DECEIT I, II, III
WHAT BAD BITCHES DO I, II, III
SOUL OF A MONSTER I II III
KILL ZONE
A DOPE BOY'S QUEEN I II III
By **Aryanna**
A KINGPIN'S AMBITON
A KINGPIN'S AMBITION **II**
I MURDER FOR THE DOUGH
By **Ambitious**
TRUE SAVAGE I II III IV V VI VII
DOPE BOY MAGIC I, II, III
MIDNIGHT CARTEL I II III
CITY OF KINGZ I II
NIGHTMARE ON SILENT AVE
THE PLUG OF LIL MEXICO II

By **Chris Green**
A DOPEBOY'S PRAYER
By **Eddie "Wolf" Lee**
THE KING CARTEL **I, II & III**
By **Frank Gresham**
THESE NIGGAS AIN'T LOYAL **I, II & III**
By **Nikki Tee**
GANGSTA SHYT **I II &III**
By **CATO**

246

The Billionaire Bentleys

THE ULTIMATE BETRAYAL
By **Phoenix**
BOSS'N UP **I , II & III**
By **Royal Nicole**
I LOVE YOU TO DEATH
By **Destiny J**
I RIDE FOR MY HITTA
I STILL RIDE FOR MY HITTA
By **Misty Holt**
LOVE & CHASIN' PAPER
By **Qay Crockett**
TO DIE IN VAIN
SINS OF A HUSTLA
By **ASAD**
BROOKLYN HUSTLAZ
By **Boogsy Morina**
BROOKLYN ON LOCK I & II
By **Sonovia**
GANGSTA CITY
By **Teddy Duke**
A DRUG KING AND HIS DIAMOND I & II III
A DOPEMAN'S RICHES
HER MAN, MINE'S TOO I, II
CASH MONEY HO'S
THE WIFEY I USED TO BE I II
By Nicole Goosby
TRAPHOUSE KING **I II & III**

Von Diesel

KINGPIN KILLAZ I II III

STREET KINGS I II

PAID IN BLOOD **I II**

CARTEL KILLAZ I II III

DOPE GODS I II

By **Hood Rich**

LIPSTICK KILLAH **I, II, III**

CRIME OF PASSION I II & III

FRIEND OR FOE I II III

By **Mimi**

STEADY MOBBN' **I, II, III**

THE STREETS STAINED MY SOUL I II III

By **Marcellus Allen**

WHO SHOT YA **I, II, III**

SON OF A DOPE FIEND I II

HEAVEN GOT A GHETTO

Renta

GORILLAZ IN THE BAY **I II III IV**

TEARS OF A GANGSTA I II

3X KRAZY I II

STRAIGHT BEAST MODE

DE'KARI

TRIGGADALE I II III

MURDAROBER WAS THE CASE

Elijah R. Freeman

GOD BLESS THE TRAPPERS I, II, III

THESE SCANDALOUS STREETS I, II, III

248

The Billionaire Bentleys

FEAR MY GANGSTA I, II, III IV, V

THESE STREETS DON'T LOVE NOBODY I, II

BURY ME A G I, II, III, IV, V

A GANGSTA'S EMPIRE I, II, III, IV

THE DOPEMAN'S BODYGAURD I II

THE REALEST KILLAZ I II III

THE LAST OF THE OGS I II III

Tranay Adams

THE STREETS ARE CALLING

Duquie Wilson

MARRIED TO A BOSS I II III

By Destiny Skai & Chris Green

KINGZ OF THE GAME I II III IV V VI

Playa Ray

SLAUGHTER GANG I II III

RUTHLESS HEART I II III

By Willie Slaughter

FUK SHYT

By Blakk Diamond

DON'T F#CK WITH MY HEART I II

By Linnea

ADDICTED TO THE DRAMA I II III

IN THE ARM OF HIS BOSS II

By Jamila

YAYO I II III IV

A SHOOTER'S AMBITION I II

BRED IN THE GAME

Von Diesel

The Billionaire Bentleys

By **Malik D. Rice**

LIFE OF A SAVAGE I II III

A GANGSTA'S QUR'AN I II III IV

MURDA SEASON I II III

GANGLAND CARTEL I II III

CHI'RAQ GANGSTAS I II III

KILLERS ON ELM STREET I II III

JACK BOYZ N DA BRONX I II III

A DOPEBOY'S DREAM I II III

JACK BOYS VS DOPE BOYS

By **Romell Tukes**

LOYALTY AIN'T PROMISED I II

By **Keith Williams**

QUIET MONEY I II III

THUG LIFE I II III

EXTENDED CLIP I II

By **Trai'Quan**

THE STREETS MADE ME I II III

By **Larry D. Wright**

THE ULTIMATE SACRIFICE I, II, III, IV, V, VI

KHADIFI

IF YOU CROSS ME ONCE

ANGEL I II

IN THE BLINK OF AN EYE

By **Anthony Fields**

THE LIFE OF A HOOD STAR

By **Ca$h & Rashia Wilson**

Von Diesel

THE STREETS WILL NEVER CLOSE I II
By K'ajji
CREAM I II
THE STREETS WILL TALK
By Yolanda Moore
NIGHTMARES OF A HUSTLA I II III
By King Dream
CONCRETE KILLA I II
VICIOUS LOYALTY
By Kingpen
HARD AND RUTHLESS I II
MOB TOWN 251
THE BILLIONAIRE BENTLEYS I II III
By Von Diesel
GHOST MOB
Stilloan Robinson
MOB TIES I II III IV V
By SayNoMore
BODYMORE MURDERLAND I II III
By Delmont Player
FOR THE LOVE OF A BOSS
By C. D. Blue
MOBBED UP I II III IV
THE BRICK MAN I II III
THE COCAINE PRINCESS I II
By King Rio
KILLA KOUNTY I II III

The Billionaire Bentleys

By Khufu
MONEY GAME I II
By Smoove Dolla
A GANGSTA'S KARMA I II
By FLAME
KING OF THE TRENCHES I II
by **GHOST & TRANAY ADAMS**
QUEEN OF THE ZOO
By **Black Migo**
GRIMEY WAYS
By Ray Vinci
XMAS WITH AN ATL SHOOTER
By Ca$h & Destiny Skai
KING KILLA
By Vincent "Vitto" Holloway
BETRAYAL OF A THUG
By Fre$h

Von Diesel

BOOKS BY LDP'S CEO, CA$H

TRUST IN NO MAN

TRUST IN NO MAN 2

TRUST IN NO MAN 3

BONDED BY BLOOD

SHORTY GOT A THUG

THUGS CRY

THUGS CRY 2

THUGS CRY 3

TRUST NO BITCH

TRUST NO BITCH 2

TRUST NO BITCH 3

TIL MY CASKET DROPS

RESTRAINING ORDER

RESTRAINING ORDER 2

IN LOVE WITH A CONVICT

LIFE OF A HOOD STAR

XMAS WITH AN ATL SHOOTER

The Billionaire Bentleys

CPSIA information can be obtained
at www.ICGtesting.com
Printed in the USA
LVHW022048210522
719400LV00012B/640

9 781955 270991